T0198943

THE
WESTERNERS

MARK ANDERSON

authorHOUSE®

AuthorHouse™
1663 Liberty Drive
Bloomington, IN 47403
www.authorhouse.com
Phone: 1 (800) 839-8640

Published by AuthorHouse 10/20/2018

ISBN: 978-1-5462-6363-0 (sc)
ISBN: 978-1-5462-6362-3 (e)

Library of Congress Control Number: 2018912049

CHAPTER 1

HOME FROM THE CREEK

Late Saturday Afternoon June 1993 Sterling Silver quickly turns into the drive at his rural home stopping the light blue 1989 Chevy S-10 pickup right at the porch's door. Opening the pickup's door he grabs the Winchester model 9422 magnum lever action rifle and quickly steps into the porch opening the door into the den. "Charlene, Charlene!" Pulling his tan straw stethson off, while wiping dust mixed with sweat off his forehead.

"Sterling, darling," she answers, walking from the kitchen. "I've been worried about you. Look at you. Looks like something been wrastling you around. Oh no, you didn't--------

Interrupting, trying to come up with something other than actually getting a little turned around when he left the creek after fishing. How in the world did I get off the trail, I'll never know. "Well, I was on my way out with a stringer of catfish, when some creature began stalking me. Following silently the scent of the fish I'm assuming. When it got into striking distance what ever it was, hit like a train, grabbing my fish. Just sent me rolling down through a thicket of birar's and thorns. Think it could've been that lion. Lost my rifle during the attack. Happened so quick I didn't have time to use it. Took most of the afternoon to find it."

"Aw come on, My dear Sterling," she said. "Just shorten your explanation to I got lost for a while, and happened to run out of the forest about a mile from my pickup."

No body but me, no body but me, n-----o boooby but me. How she figures me out I don't know. "I've got to clean my rifle. Um, ah we are having fried chicken?"

"Yes it won't be too much longer and it'll be done. About to make the gravy for the rice when these last couple of thighs are done. Also got a mess of feild peas. I thought you would be hungry, when you come in. If I didn't have to get a couple of the deacons to go out and search for you."

Sterling said, "funny, thats just funny Lucy. ha, ha, ha. I'm going to get cleaned up and ready for supper, then clean my rifle." Charlene sets the table while Sterling is in the shower. After he finished showering, he emerges from the bathroon in a pair of short pants and white tee shirt. Entering the dinning room re-ling, reling, re-ling.

Charlene said, "go ahead and sit down I'll get the phone. Hello."

"Hi Charlee.' Milton Foxx said.

"Hi, Milton, hows things going?"

"Everything seems to be ok, just fine."

"Thats good. I know you're looking for Sterling."

"Yes. Is he close by? Or out in the wilderness?"

"He is right here just getting ready to eat dinner. hold on. Ster-------"

"Oh no Charlee, don't let me interupt ya'll's dinner. I'll call back later."

"Milton it is alright, Sterling is right here. Its for you."

Sterling pushes his chair out from the table and walks to the living room. "I'm coming, I'm a coming."

Charlene hands him the phone receiver, "it's Milton."

Sterling acknowledges, "thank you. Hello Milt, whats up?"

"Hey Sterling. We sure do miss you at the chicken plant. We the employees in the department was just talking about you the other day. Wish you were still with us. Hope all is well with you and Charlee. She still having those headaches?"

"You know Milt, I do miss ya'll too, but not the work. Ole Ken Leavenworth, was making me do more than what I was getting paid to do. I just got tired of it, and found this Job at Kuhlman."

"I'm really glad for you, and yes ken had you going. And didn't make any of the others do that either."

"Yep I have a better job and not so stressful and stregient. Charlene has the headaches but not as often. I hope her medicine is being effective. She has a doctor appointment next Thursday. I think they are going to do some test, and hopefully find out what is causing them. Sometimes they really make her sick. Hopefully Doc. Bellows will find the culprit. But right now she is doing good. Hey what about you and Burt? I assume ya'll are still in the leadership with the cub Scouts."

"Yep, we are, and they sure are a special group of kids."

"yes they are, and your son Milt Junior will be old enough to get in this year right?

"Sure will, and looking foward in helping him earn those badges."

"How is Ann doing? How old is Joni? She is what terrible two or so years old?"

"Oh yes, three. Making her just like me. And Milt is a little jealous from time to time. But thats just expected. He has been the only child, for about three years. So now that he has joined the cub scouts, maybe that'll be just what he needs. Plus be with his dad at the meetings. Oh and speaking of meetings. We just had one a couple of days ago. We are going to be working on the camping badge. But we want something different. The boys want to get off the scout reservation and those scout camporees. Since we all know you, and how experienced you are in camping. Well the wild out door world, I was elected to speak with you about maybe taking us out for a night in the wilderness. You know we've never been on a real wild camp experience. Would you happen to be free next weekend?"

"Milt, ole buddy, ole pal, you've contacted the right person. I'd be more'n glad to. In fact honored to lead a scout troop on an over night camp out. What about next Friday, and return Saturday. You know I go to church on Sunday. It wouldn't be respecting to Charlene as she is the music director. Plus I am a Sunday school teacher." So hope you can take a vacation day next Friday. You and ole Burt. I'm on vacation leave all next week. So Friday would be good for me."

"Yes thats what we had planned for. Most of the scouts are in church too. So what time do we meet?"

"Milt, just what do you have in mind? I need some specifics. A long or short hike. Ya'll want a long hike or short. Through the woods or along some road, down on the creek on the sandbar. Maybe wade through dense swamp, with cottonmouths hanging off cypress limbs like sausage in a smoke house. With a mist of thick fog rising off the damp forest floor. I need to know the specifics. Sometimes feel like swamp gas is suffocating you. See, that will give me a good idea for the trip."

"We are wanting a distance hike in varying senics as hills, woods, and to camp on a sandbar by the creek. We want that way back camp out experience. And we'd like it with a western flair. Roasting hotdogs. Heating up some chili in a pot by the fire. And of course roasting marshmallows to top it off. The scouts have new pup tents they want to try out. It'll make'em feel like troops in a calvary. Besides they want to fish and play in the creek. But we'll need some idea of how to get the supplies down to the camp site in advance. Coolers filled with iced over soft drinks and water. Other coolers will contain the food items. We would want to leave hiking early enough for us to arrive at the campsite, with plenty of day light to get set up and do some fishing and playing in the creek. Reckon, you might have an idea on how to get the supplies to the camp site?"

"Don't worry about that Milt, here is what I can do. Early Friday morning, I'll borrow Jared's atv and take the provisions to the camp site. You and Burt bring the hotdogs and drinks packed in a couple of ice chests over here late Thursday afternoon. Be sure they are packed in plenty of ice now. We'll strap them to the atv. Early Friday mornig I'll take them to the camp site down on the sandbar of Bayou Pierrie creek. Down behind the deer camp. Ya'll and the troops meet Charlene at the scout hut. She'll drive ya'll to the deer camp where I'll be waiting, by eleven o'clock. Aw shoot!"

"What."

"Oh well, never mind. I can fill all of ya'll in on safety precautions Friday morning at the dropping off point."

"All right, we'll see you Thursday afternoon. Thanks alot."

"Okay good bye."

Charlene said, "I take it that Milt and Burt wants you to take them and the scouts on a camping trip. Come on and sit down I have the table set now. I'm hungry, lets eat."

Sitting down at the table Sterling commented. "Hey it sure smells great." As he dips the table spoon into the bowl of peas. Then he pricks a chicken breast with the fork. Then gets into the rice covering the dish with gravy, he glances up at Charlene, as she is getting a serving of peas.

"Thank you honey. I hope it is good. How about lets have the blessing before we eat?"

"Yes, we shall.--a-men.

Sterling taking a fork full of peas, Charlene ask. "So what about it? When is this camping trip to take place?"

Charlene biting into a thigh. Sterling looking up to her, while wiping his hands on a napkin and then raises it to his mouth. "I'm taking them out Friday afternoon, and return Saturday about mid day. Yep, they want to go on a hiking campout. They are working on their camping badge. First one this year. I'm gonna give them an experience that will stick with them for a long time to come. Might get famous for it."

Charlene wiping her hands and mouth from the chicken and then a sample of the rice and gravy. "Think I put a little too much salt in the gravy."

"Oh noooo you didn't got it just right. It is really good." Looking at the build up of bones on his plate. "I'm full, I enjoyed that, thank you baby."

"Thank you honey, I'm going to get the dishes cleaned up and then get in the bed. Maybe read a little. Got to get up early and get to church and go over the special I'm singing. Then I can be in the Sunday School class incase you need some help teaching. So you are needing me to take the scouts out to the camp Friday morning?" She gets up and walks to the kitchen sink and turns the water on. Sterling rises as she returns to get their plates. "I'll take it Sterling."

"Charlene, baby, I'll be more-n glad to help. I'll dry the dishes for ya."

"No, Sterling, I've got'em. Won't take long. Just tell me what are you planning for those boys. Just don't scare'em too bad.

"Sterling sits down in a kitchen table chair, explaining. "Aw, I'm gonna get them excited a bit. Ain't no camping trip without excitment. You know they want a western style outing so they'll get one, complete with wild west indians, and they just might get scalped."

"Now Sterling, honey, don't scare those kids too bad. Be easy with them on the hike. You know Milt is'nt a picture of fitness, with his expanding waist. If he doesn't watch it he will be as wide as he is tall. What around five and a quarter feet. You know he'll believe anything you tell him. Why he looks to you Sterling for encouragement."

"But Charlene, my dearest, they will survive and have an experience to tell the whole outfit about. Other troops may want me to lead them on a camp out too. I wouldn't worry about ole Milt and Burt, They'll be just fine. You know I was picking at Burt one day before I quit that chicken factory. I said Burt, I see you are getting taller in your mid thirties. He told me I'm not getting taller. What makes you think I'm growing? I done all my growing years ago. Most if not all of my growth seemed to happen in my teens. I'm knocking on the door of my forties now and I really don't feel I'm getting taller. I've been six foot three inches since those teens. I may need to lose some weight as I'm closing in on a hundred and seventy five pounds. So what gives you the impression that I'm getting taller? We---l--l, I said, I thought you was. Because the top of your head is growing up through your hair. Alright Tim Conway, he replied. So what I'm losing some of my hair. I'm going to start the rogaine treatment."

"ha, ha, ha. You know I don't think either of them has much of a sense of humor."

"Aw, they're alright, if I didn't like em I wouldn't pick on them. And they do take picking in stride. They know me, they know how I am. Thats why they always look to me. Friday morning when I take the provisions to the camp site I'm going to set my out door theater system speakers up and let them hear the lion growl. Then right at dark they'll hear that dreaded swamp gnat. I think maybe I'll mix up some gnat repellant."

Finishing the dishes, she walks to the table and sits down in a chair. "Now Sterling darling let me tell you one thing. What ever you do don't get any of that stuff on you. I'm telling ya, you won't be allowed back in the house for weeks or months. Remember the winters are cold. You ain't coming in here and will not get a blanket or quilt to cover up with. I don't know what you use to make that stuff, but it is more than terrible. Those kids are going to be stinking, well more than stinking should you talk them into putting that stuff on. I really don't think you should go that far. Now Milton and Burt if they do, it's on them, if they are that gullible."

Standing up looking at the gun room. Then quickly looking back at Charlene, then glancing again toward the room. "It'll take a couple of months to wear off, provided they don't get wet. It is a concoction I developed myself. It contains the glandular musk of a pole cat, mixed with a couple bottles of doe deer in heat sent, with a buck's tarsal gland soaking in the pee. Let it brew about twenty four hours then add a couple drops of spirits of ammonia to power this stuff. Now this will not only repel gnats, but any thing else you might want repelled. The neighbors from miles around might decide to take an extended vacation."

"Look Sterling, do not get it on you. Repellant, swamp gnats, escaped lion, ha. I'm heading to the bathroom to brush my teeth and then to the bedroom. Good night Sterling, I love you."

"Good night, I'll be on to bed when I get my gun cleaned and get myself brushed up too. I love you too."

"Oh, I'll leave the night light on should, I get through reading, and turn the lamp off. Again good night."

"Good night, I'll probably be on to bed before you turn out the light." Sterling cleans the Winchester model ninety four twenty two caliber magnum rifle and returns it back to it's place in the gun cabinet. For a moment he sits down at his reloading and study bench, opens a drawer retreving the Sunday school book he will be teaching from, and reviews the lesson, for a while. Then enters the bedroon, just as Charlene is about to turn her lamp off.

"Oh, Sterling I set the alarm clock for six, Don't let me over sleep. I need to be at the church by eight thirty, to run through the special music one last time."

"I'll be sure you're up. I know you are going to do great baby. I like the way you are so professional."

Well Sterling you know the Lord gave his best for us. I want to give him my best. And I try to teach the choir those same qualities, and really try to work with them on singing. It is something I love to do."

She reaches up to turn the lamp off lays down, looks over at Sterling and gives him a kiss. "Lets get some sleep."

Buzz, buzz, buzz, buzz. "Charlene wake up. Turn that thing off."

"Okay, okay, she reaches for the clock. Seems like we just laid down a few minutes ago. Its six o'clock already. Better get up now."

"I'm going to make coffee and get the day started." As Charlene staggers through the bed room on her way to the bathroom. Sliding her hand through the tangled hair.

"I'll get it started and then go up to McDonalds and get us a sausage-n-bisquit." He dresses, "Okay baby I'll be back in a few minutes."

"Hey, I want the muffin egg, bacon, and cheese. Be careful."

Walking back into their home, Charlene sits two steaming cups on the table, and Sterling opens the bag of breakfast. "Thank you for going and getting breakfast honey. I'm going to finish getting dressed. Don't come into the bathroom until I'm dressed. Then you can have it when I go back into the bedroom."

"Alright baby, I won't disturb you. All I've got to do is shave and put my sweet smell on, Millionaire. I'm going in my gun room and go over that lesson a few minutes." Sterling pours another cup of coffee and sits down at his bench. Props his head in his hands and has a prayer and then opens the book to the lesson.

Knock, knock, knock, "Sterling I'm out of the bathroom. We may need to get a move on. It won't take me long to get myself all prettied up."

"I'm gone to get shaved, and get my shirt and tie on. I'll be ready before you are."

"All right you trying to get something started you can't finish?" Sterling takes one last look in the mirror to make sure his tie is up neat and straight. Then opens the door, to a sight that causes him to take a step back. "Wow! Charlene look at you!"

"I thought you would like it." As she spins around. "Like it?"

"Why baby you know what your style is." She walks toward him.

Man this is a bueatiful woman in this sky pink skirt, and white blouse. Admiring her bueaty, light pink lipstick, nail polish and other various makeup items, she blends together to get that wow look. Along with her long flowing reddish brown hair, that twists and curls along it's length, making her seem taller than she actually is of around five foot five inches and no more-n- a hundred pounds. Sterling stands there in awe as he looks into her hazel eyes, and one more step she gives him a hug. Sterling then puckers up for the kiss he's expecting. "No Sterling, ain't messing my lipstick up. Come on it is time to go to the church. I want to go over the special I'm singing today, and still make it to the Sunday school class, you'll be teaching. Hey good looking man, I'm so in love with you. Honey you know I love you."

"Lets go, I'll help you in the practice run. And I love you too darling."

At the closing of the service Reverend Stockon said, "And remember, enter to worship, depart to serve. Thank you all for your attendance, and hope to see you again this evening. Maybe, if enough of you Christians who enjoyed Charlene's message in music will come back, maybe she'll sing it again. Again thank you sister Charlene for your musical talents you serve here with us. That was a glorious song you sung."

Charlene said, "thank you brother Stockon I enjoyed singing it and was to bring worship, honor and glory to my saviour Jesus Christ. He is the reason I love to sing. Give God the glory and praise."

Reverend Stockon said, "To make it fitting, I'll ask Brother Sterling to close with a prayer. And Ya'll let Charlene know how well she did." And above all we pray to you oh God, we thank you for your mercy and Salvation and it is in the name of Jesus our Lord and Saviour, a-men.

Sterling immediately turns to Charlene and said "Charlene, baby I really enjoyed that song and how you put the feeling and emotions in it."

As others are approaching them Sterling quickly hugs her, and she then puckers up for a quick kiss, but Sterling said, "don't want to mess your lipstick up. ha, ha, ha, ha,."

"Aren't you plum comical." Other members and guest are commenting and congradulating her for a fine song. And a couple of guest are wanting to invite her for Sunday concerts. And leaving their contact information. Then Jared and Mona comes to them, with encouragements to Charlene. Jared said, "You nailed it Sister."

Sterling asked, "Jared, will you loan me your four wheeler Friday morning?"

"Sure as long as you won't get lost out there somewhere. You going fishing?"

"Naw I'm leading Milt and Burt's scout troops on a out back campout. I just need transportation for a couple of ice chests filled with food and cold drinks. It is an over nighter. You know playing and fishing in the creek, then build a camp fire to roast hot dogs and marshmallows. Then tell some ghost stories. Thursday morning I'll come over and get it. I told Milt and Burt to bring their stuff over to my house and we'd load it on. Then Friday morning I'll take the provisions to the camp site. Charlene will meet the scouts at the hut or headquarters. They'll meet her there and she'll drive them to the dropping off point, where they will meet me."

"Sure you can. Come on over and get it Thursday."

"Sterling expresses his grattitude, then said we're going to Knues for lunch."

Charlene said "Thats where we are going. Yall wanna go with us?" "How about just meetiing us there."

When the church is cleared, She turns to Sterling again and said "alright I don't mind mess ing the lipstick up," as they then kiss quickly. Charlene said, "Lets go to Knue's for lunch." They walk out the front door shaking hands with Reverend Stockon, a tall slim black haired man, with black rimmed glasses.

Sterling said, "Brother Billy that was a great sermon. We'll see you tonight."

"Thank you, Sterling it is what the Lord laid on my heart this week, to preach." Looking at Charlene, "reckon you could sing that song again tonight?"

"Sure I would love to. It's what I'm called to do." As a ghostly demoralizing thought rises up from from a haunting grave. But she tries to put it back down and breathes a silent prayer for it to be dismissed, while walking arm in arm with Sterling. He opens the door of the Chevy S-10 pickup and she gets in with a "thank you."

CHAPTER 2

DINNER IS DONE

"Sterling, baby I have dinner on the table waiting. come on out of your gun room and share dinner with me. Barbequed chicken breast, baked beans, and potato salad."

"I'm coming honey, it sure smells good", as he enters the kitchen. "I've got to wash up you know, be right back."

"I just made a half gallon of sweet tea, or do you want coke?"

As he is washing his hands he shouts to Charlene. "I want your sweet tea and put no more that five ice cubes, in my glass."

"Already itching for a brusing." Hum, he thinks he is in charge, thats funny. As she pours him a glass of tea with exalty five cubes floating in it. Returning to the kitchen table he slides out her chair waiting, slieghs a hand, for her to sit down. He reaches over kissing her cheek saying. "Thank you for dinner, it looks good." He saunters to his end of the table and sits down taking the towel spreading it out over his right thigh. Then they lean foward to each other clasping hands Sterling leads the prayer of thankfulnes and says "a-men."

"Ok baby dive on in, before it get any colder," Sterling sticking a fork into a breast then dips a serving of potato salad, and baked beans.

Cutting a bite size chunck of meat taking it in as he tastes the slight sweet tang of the sauce, instantly reaches for a glass of tea. "I thought you said it was cool."

"No, baby, I said before it cools down." As she dips a serving of baked beans. "Are you still planning to take the scouts out Friday night?"

"Well I'm planning on it." Wiping his hands and mouth. I'm waiting for Milt to call me. If he does'nt call me I'm not. Since I've already taken off from work tomorrow and Friday, I'm planning on going out and get some photographs of the lake in early morning. And just wander around taking a few photos. Might go fishing in the creek Saturday. Unless you have something planned. It sure was hard to get a couple of vacation days approved. They just don't like it when I want a couple of days off. Always busy and staying behind. Plus don't no body else wants to pull and beat that cable through those coils." Taking a fork of potato salad.

"Um," pulling a breast apart, "all I have planned is to go for a doctor's appointment tomorrow morning. Just a check up and get my medicine scripts renewed. My headaches seems to want to start up again with a vengence. Sterling, now just please bear with me if I get sarcastic again at times and cumbersome to get along with. It's not me, those achs are so bad they keep me feeling bad. And I just need quiteness."

Ring-ring-ring, "I'll get it baby, sit there and finish eating." Hello, Yes Milt, he was just talking about and looking for your call. He'll be right on. Ya'll still going out with ole Wild Sterling Silver? Spect ya'll a come back crying bye ole Silver, instead of high, ole silver." chuckling.

"Milt asked "what ya mean by that?"

Charlene said, "Aw come on Milt, don't be so nervous, Just kidding a little."

MIlt replied. "Well you know when he comes back from a venture of his own, it for the most part ends in some kind of ordeal. And Burt is a bit concerned too."

Charlene asked, "Milt, have you ever seen any scratches or really deep cuts and puncture wounds on ole Silver? If any at all, were from brairs scratching him when he run through a thicket in panic from being lost, well turned around. Ain't never spent more-n-one night out in the wilderness. Ya'll ain't got a thing to worry about."

"Milt said, "you know Charlie, you're right, come to think about it. And most of his over night sequals was planned. Always had you with him."

Charlene replied, "Yep Milt when I go with him it is always a wonderful experience. Wouldn't want to be in any one else's ar-um protection. Here is Wild West Silver."

Milt calling, "Charlie, Charlie."

Charlene answering, "Yes Milt."

Milt said, "Thank you for the assurance. It'll be welcome news to Burt and the troop. I have a preparedness meeting in about an hour."

Charlene said, "Ya'll ain't got a thing to worry about. Now here is Ole Silver."

Sterling taking the phone grinning at Charlene, wispering, "good one."

Sterling said, "high Milt ole buddy ole pal, been wondering if you was going to call."

Milt said, "Sterling, you are planning on leading us aren't you?"

"Sure am, Milt, wouldn't miss it for the world. I'm going to get Jared's atv tomorrow morning, and drive it back over here. Thats how I'm going to get the main supplies to camp. Just bring the supplies over here tomorrow afternoon when ya'll get off work. Have every thing packed on ice. We'll tie em down on the rack."

"Ok I have a preparedness meeting in about forty five minutes. I'll let Burt know. Any thing about the schedule I need to bring up at this meeting?"

"Well Milt, you don't even have a schedule yet except to bring the supplies over here. So tell them I'm going to take those food and drink supplies to the camp site Friday morning. You, Burt and the troopers meet Charlene at the scout hut around 10:00 am. Be sure the troopers know they will be responsible to pack their back packs with bed rolls tied on them, along with their tents. And what ever else ya'll want to pack. And I'll meet ya'll at the dropping off point, deer camp around 10:30 am. See ya'll tomorrow afternoon."

Oh yea, I do need to bring up the itenary, don't I. So 10:00 am at the scout hut. Charlie will take us to the camp. You'll meet us there around 10:30 am. We'll return to the dropping off point around noon Saturday. So the parents can plan to meet them at the scout hut around 12:30 pm."

"Yep, thats it Milt be sure to let them know."

"I will, and we are looking foward to it, see you tomorrow around 6:00pm or there bouts. Good bye."

"Good bye. Oh! wait, ah never mind. We'll have our own meeting Friday morning at the dropping off point, I can inform every one then."

"Wha-what is it?"

"Aw nothing much right now, you know insect spray. I'm sure ya'll are aware of biting insects, and similar things."

"Oh, thats all? We'll have that. It is what the meeting is about. See you tomorrow. Good bye."

"Good bye."

"Well Charlene, the trip is set. Hey I enjoyed the dinner."

"I've just about got every thing cleaned up and going to the shower. Don't have to get up so early tomorrow morning. We'll watch that western movie coming on. Got one of my medical days off from work."

"What time is your appointment?"

"At 9:45 am."

After the movie ends, Charlene said, "well I enjoyed that one for a change. I'm off to bed honey. Set the clock for around 6:30 am will ya?"

"I will. I'm going to watch the news and weather, then I'll be on. Hey I will go with you if you want me to."

"Not really, you've got to get that atv, and prepare yourself for the outing. Its just a check up. Plus I'm going shopping when I get off. Got a special day coming up. You know it wouldn't hurt for you to get a checkup too."

"Will you make a appointment for me when you see doctor Bellows?"

"Sure, won't be any problem. She kisses him, "Good night. I love you."

"Good night, I love you too."

Buzz, buzz, buzz. Then the radio announcer came on the air. "That was KC and the Sunshine band. The sun is up and you too need to get up. Up next to get you going is Dolly Pardon nine to five. So get up and going."

Sterling! Turn that thing off."

"I'm trying, I'm tryng." Fumbling for the snooze button, turning it off for a few more moments. *Buzz, buzz, buzz.* Reaching out to the radio alarm, finally turning it off. "Ok, ok, I'm getting up. I'm going to make coffee." He walks to the bathroom, washes his hands and face, then to the kitchen. Coffee starts brewing as he walks to the front door opening it to greet the new day. Going to be pretty warm today. Then closes the door returns to the kitchen and pours himself a cup of coffee, then sits down at the table. Charlene staggers by on her way to the bathroom, sliding a hand through her tangled hair.

"Good morning baby. Coffee sure smells good."

"Good morning, I'll have you a cup when you come out. Want some eggs and bacon?"

"Um no, just coffee. be back in a minute." She returns to the kitchen wanders to the table sitting down. taking a sip of coffee. Then props up on her hands and slides them through her hair. Yawns and takes another sip. "Sure is good." After sipping a couple of cups down. "I'm going to get dressed and ready to go and see Doctor Bellows. Then like I said I'm going shopping. Be gone most of the day unless I get a head ache. I'll bring dinner home for tonight. What would you like?

Sterling gets up and pours himself another cup. "Well I don't know. Long Johns Silvers, the fish and chicken combo. Naw, there is the Chinese resturant, my favorite there is the Almond duck. Aw shoot wait a second maybe a three peice dinner box from KFC, original receipe. Just surprise me with one of these."

"Alright then, I'll surprise you honey. I've got to get myself ready and all prettied up. Before I leave we'll have our Spiritual devotion and prayer. Then I'll be off to greet the day."

Sterling slips into his sporting and gun room, looking around. He gazes at the mounted ten point buck adorning the wall. Walks to it staring it in the eyes as his memory carries him back a number of years ago at the deer camp. He drew a stand near the creek, that was known to be a good spot it was aptly named, The Good Spot. He got in there early just in case he might get one slipping out ahead of the other standers coming in. But it wasn't to be. About an hour later the dogs howled out in a loud high pitch hot on a deer. He was alert and ready, but the deer turned away from him taking the chase back into the hills. A few shots from different locations sounded off through the frozen wilderness. At the point of the last location the chase ended. Standing there shaking from the frigid tempature, and excitment of the chase, he was shivering, noticing his breath floating upwards in a white vapor. Sunlight sprinkling the frosty forest, with little warmth. Frozen feet felt like standing on pins and needles. But dared to move, looking for one trying to slip out. All of a sudden the howling and barking of hounds rose above the hills. Hey, the thought entered into his mind. Those hounds are headed this way. That deer has gained some distance from them. Then the crackling of leaves and and small sticks breaking, stirring his alertness. He had the deer pinpointed and where he would appear in the hardwood creek bottom. Anywhere within that fifty or seventy five yards the deer would be in open woods. Then quietness, and all he could hear was the barking hounds racing into the creek bottom. As they arrived closer and still no deer, he wondered if the deer had gotten by him. When out of no where it seemed the buck broke into a gallop trying to cross the open forested bottom and cross the creek. Sterling saw the shiny antlers and mounted the Remington 11-87, swinging the white bead ahead of the buck and pulled the trigger. At the shot Sterling noticed the buck seemed to be struck with an electic shock, as the body shook. But he seemed to speed up as Sterling kept tracking em with the bead just ahead of his body, firing and the buck tumbled at the next load of #00 buck shot. Coming back to the moment easing over to a mounted red fox squirrel so big, he actually thought for a moment it was a fox on the log. He quickly identified it as what it was and put a .22mag hollow point into the shoulder. I should'nt have killed that old animal. I knew he was old by the white nose and face when I viewed him through the four power scope. But it was a rather long shot. He finally comes back to focus on the commitment at hand. To prepare a scout troop for an adventure of a life time. He opens a trunk containing his out door theater system. Plugging the cord into the outlet and quickly hooking the speakers up, he places one of his tapes in for inspection. With the volume turned down he listens as a smile comes across his face. While it is playing a recording of the MGM iconic lion roaring, just before a movie comes on. He plugs the battery charger up for a quick charge. Then a segment comes on that he had forgotten about. Hey maybe I can use that too. Knock, knock, knock, Sterling turns the stero off saying "come on in." Then the door opens, and Sterling just melts at the sight.

In a high pitched and low voice. "Hi baby. How do I look?"

"Why are you asking me? You know you look fine darling." *Wow!* the thought enters his mind. Man, that little black sleeveless dress, her makeup, the lively reddish blonde hair all bouncy. She slowly makes her way to him. Taking in the gleaming hazel eyes And she is coming to me. "Why you look stunning. Can I go with you?"

She gives him a hug saying, "come on back into the kitchen and lets have one more cup of coffee before we depart for the day. She brings him a steaming cup to the table. Yep I dress for you baby. When people see me in public I want them to see me, the wife of Sterling. Its Esencential to dress in respect of you. You are my husband. Sit down I'll bring you a cup. I know just the amount of sugar you want."

Sterling sits down looking at the woman, his wife bringing him a cup of coffee. I know just what our Spiritual morning worship will be about. He takes a sip, as she sits down on the side of the table, looking at him a soft smile comes across her red lips as she begins humming the The Old Rugged Cross.

"Come on honey, sing it with me. You can do it. Its time for Wor. "On A hill far------. Lifting her hands upwards, as she sings. Sterling tries to join in a little. "Ah thats it honey just let it go. as she ends the song. Might just get you up with me one Sunday to sing a duet. that would be fun. Whats our topic for devotion going to be?"

"You know I'm not going to quote or read any verses, this morning. I was just thinking about a comment you made to me a moment ago."

"What was that?"

"Well you said about why you dress the way you do. Always looking your best, and believe me you are shinning. And it makes me proud of it too."

"Well thank you honey. So how does this tie in with what you want to say?"

"For a moment just think, God gave his best to us in his Son Jesus Christ. He lived the best for us. And his best was when he rose from that grave completing Salvation for those who will accept him as their Lord and Saviour. So with the comment you made to me about your dress style in respect of me, but I also know its in respect of the Lord too. In the same way I try to dress good for you too. And as I've noticed the way some people come dressed to church just makes me cringe. And these people know they can dress better. I know that you know dress style says a lot about a person too. That is one of many ways I feel that makes God our Heavenly Father look on us proudly. Remember he looked at Job with pride or he would'nt have been bragging on him to Satan. So in hopes of making God proud it actually brings glory and honor to him. When I'm seen in public I want to look as good as I can too. And yes I like my jeans as well as dress clothes too. But it's all in how we present them, both to God and humans.

So now lets pray. And we thank you dear Lord for being with us today, in Jesus name a-men."

"And a-men. And our personal relationship with each other relflects on our personal relationship with the Lord. And our appearence can make or break that first impression of people we come across in public. Well Sterling honey its about time for me to go to doctor Bellows. I won't be too late coming home. I'll bring a suprise dinner for us tonight. Have fun with your outdoor toys today and give Jared and Mona my regards. I love you my man."

"I will, and I love you too." Sterling finishes the coffee. Man I better get dressed, myself and get over to Mona and Jared's home, before they leave. He walks across the road to their house, stepping up on the porch he pushes the door bell several times.

CHAPTER 3

SCOUT'S MOTTO

Jared rushes to the door "Ok Sterling I hear you. I'm a coming, I'm a coming. Opening the door "I know you are here, come on in. entering the large living room of their brick home.

Sterling said, "Ah quiet comfortable in here."

"Gonna be hot today and June isn't over with yet, then July sure nough gets hot. sit down." He sits down on the brown leather sofa. The Today show was concluding.

"Well Jared how is the modeling business going?" Glancing around the room.

"I really like it. It is fun to pose in all those camoflauged hunting clothes, boots and hats, for the hunters out there. then pose in the fancy fishing outfits for the fishermen. It is quite extensive. outfitter style, African safaris as well as travel outfits, for voyages on the ocean. It is an endless business. Why don't you give it a try? I could help you."

"It seems to me that would be an enveious occupation. But you have a knack and body to pull that posing off. You are about six feet and a couple of inches. Don't know your weight but it seems in line with your occupation. And you seem to have iconic face and features that gets agents all stirred up about." I'll think about it next week, but right now I have to keep a committment I made to Milton and Burt. of course we should be back home safely in a few days."

"Ha, ha, ha, ha that would be something if you got them lost."

"Thought about it but don't think I'll do it. Moms and dads are going to be surprised and even angry when they all return."

How is Charlene doing? She made a hit in church last Sunday. That woman knows music, with a voice to go with it."

"She is gone to a doctor appointment with doc. Bellows. So I fugured I would mosey right on over to get the atv before ya'll left."

"Well Mona has a great singing voice too. In fact back a couple of weeks ago when they sung that duet, Mrs. Parkinson remarked that they sounded like the angles they are. Yea, right." Sterling hears the bedroom door open and Mona coming down the blue carpeted hall.

"All right I heard that snide remark." grinning.

Sterling said. "Why Mona you look plumb like a doll. You and Charlene are the two prettiest women in Copiah county."

"Well thank you Sterling, Aren't we being sweet, today. Would you like a cup of coffee or a coke."

Sterling began chuckling and Jared trying to keep from laughing showing a little grin on his face. "Ain't nothing but a table spoon of soft sugar. If Jared is having coffee then I'll have coffee. With three teaspoons of sugar."

Mona almost five feet nine inches tall, in her highheel shoes, red dress sandy blonde fresh curled hair, mumbles to herself, "more like a lump. All right this ain't Charlene." Getting the coffee perking. Sterling walks into the kitchen sits down at the table. As Jared walks in. Before he can sit down she meets him with a kiss. "I'm heading out to the office, I love you, you bag of sugar."

Turnning a little pink in the face, then a light red to a dark red. "I love you too. Oh today I'll be on an afternoon shoot. Should be home around seven."

"Ya'll, enjoy the day. Oh love you too Sterling, but no you ain't getting a kiss." Closing the door behind her laughing.

Sterling staring at Jared asked. "Jared you gonna keep that red color?

"Just give me a few minutes will ya? And I'll be back to normal. You know she does that on purpose. She knows I'm gonna turn red. You got her started. Come on and get a cup of coffee." Sterling pours a cup and starts to sit down at the table. "Jared walks by heading to the living room. "Come on in here. Well watch the rest of the Today Show, and I'll get the atv key for ya." Sterling sits down on the sofa inspecting Jared's expression. "What are you looking at now? Whats so funny?"

"Aw nothing, we-l-l you're still a bit red." And Jared turns fiery red again.

"I knew I should'nt ev ask what you were smirking about. I should've known what it is. Yea ya'll think its funny."

When the today show ends Sterling stands up. "Well I guess I need to be going. Got other things to do later. I'll bring the four wheeler back Saturday afternoon." He hands the key to Sterling. Thank you, and enjoy the photographic ad shoot this evening."

"I will, and think about getting into this business too. I can help. good bye." Jared closes the door behind, and Sterling meanders to the garage. Visually checking the atv out and then gets on fireing it up, he drives it back home.

The tall older rounded man, with dark hair graying on both sides, enters back into the exam room, peering over his black rimmed glasses at the medical chart. Doctor Bellowes looks at Charlene. "Well Charlene it appears you're in great shape. However there is one little thing I want to futher test concerning those headaches. We'll start with targeted blood work. He finishes the requset sheet. "Okay Charlene, go right there to the lab and they'll draw a gallon or so of blood. No, no, smirking, I mean a pint. Then make an appointment two weeks from today."

Charlene asked, "What about Sterling? You told me that you needed to see him more often too."

"Yes that is right, bring him with you that same day."

"Ok Dr. Bellows, I'll get this done and then make the appointment, and we'll see you on July fifteenth. Good by.

Meanwhile at home Sterling is getting his gear prepared for a night out on the creek. Since the scouts have tents then I'll set one up too. Scrounging around in a locked chest he finds two bottles of hidden repellant. Opens a bottle and slightly takes a sniff. Throws his head back and then shakes like a deer hound. Gosh, this stuff grows in potency with time. My outdoor tape player plays great and checked in baggage. With all his equipment checked and ready to go, Sterling walks into the kitchen, opens the fridge, gathering the beef bolonga and mayonaise. With sandwich and a coke in hand he wanders out onto the porch and sits down in the swing. Swinging back and forth munching on the sandwich, he begins to lay out the plans in his mind. Looking at his watch,'um I got time to go to Wal-Mart and wander around the sporting goods department to browse around just in case I might be forgetting something, I may need later.'

"Hey Sterling", Bobby Andrews, calls from across the aisle.

"Hi Bobby, don't guess you had to work today."

"Nawp, had to take a medical day today and go to the dentist. She yanked two jaw teeth out. Waiting for my painpills to be filled and then I'm going home and lay down for a while. Betty will be home around four thirty this evening. Hope I can get some rest before she comes home. Taking tomorrow off too, a vacation day. A missed day excused or not makes for a long pay week."

"Tell me about it will ya. I took this whole week off. Ain't it funny how time speeds up when you're off work. I'm taking Milton, Burt and their cub scout troop on a hike and camping trip tomorrow. I'm just wandering around here trying to joggle my memory about a necessary item that could make or break the whole campout."

"I sure would like to go, but the way I feel right now I just want to go home."

"You sure would be welcome to go. If you get to feeling better call me." Bobby Andrews, the call came on, your prescription is ready for pick up.

"Thanks Sterling, but I'll pass on this trip. I'm going to get my medicine and go home, and lay down. I can feel the shots are wearing off. See ya later."

"Okay Bob, you'll get over this. A couple of days and this will be only a memory." Well I can't think of anything I actually need so guess I'll go back home too. Stop by Wendys and get a frosty.

He returns home, hoping Charlene would be back by now but she isn't. Opening the door he checks phone calls. However there is a couple of messages recorded for Charlene, from a couple of church choir members. Looking at his watch and the clock on kitchen wall three thirty pm as he opens the fridge retreving a coke and then walks outside and sets down on a bench looking for Charlene and then Burt and Milt. Then about forty five minutes later, while Sterling was reading the news paper Milt and Burt drives up in Burt's green Dodge powerwagen pickup. Milton stretching to get out of the tall vehicle, while Sterling approaches it. "Hey Scout troopers."

Burt shuts the big engine down and walks around the front of the pickup. Reaching out to shake hands with Sterling. "Hi Sterling, good to see you."

"Good to see you too Burt. Often I think about you, since I've left the chicen plant."

Milt ask, "Ya'll gonna help with this stuff? These ice chest are a bit heavy."

Sterling looking at Milt said. "Hold on a second. Whats the hurry? Ann got you on a time chain?"

"Noooooooo. I just want to get this stuff on the four wheeler and then we can vsit."

"Well, lets get it done. Ya" bring the supplies around back and place the chests on the rack. I'll tie em down. Ya'll sure every thing is together? Remember ain't no coming back for any forgotten items."

Burt said, "yep we have every thing together. Double and tripled checked. So I understand you have a great spot located."

"Sterling said," Yes I do it'll take about a hour and a half hike to reach it. That'll be long enough to wear on some energy."

"Sounds good to me. But." Looking at Milt then back at Sterling. "Ya'll know I'm not really the campout type. Being out amongst bugs, gnats not to mention those pesky mosquitos. Then getting all smoked up by the camp fire. Smell like smoke over a week. However I do like the experience of leading the scouts, and I know this is a requirement. I'll do the best I can on an outing of this nature. Hey almost forgot, I want to put my Zebco thirty three combo and a few lures on the atv too. Let me get it."

Sterling said. "Ok Burt I'll allow that, what about you Milt. Are you taking fishing equipment too?"

Milt answereing. "Nope, thought about it, but I just want to enjoy the experience with the kids. You know swimming and playing in the creek."

Burt said, "wait a minute, about a hour and a half hike to the camp base."

"Sterling said, "Yep maybe a little shorter, maybe a little longer, depends on the pace we'll be marching to."

Burt said, Sounds like we'll be in a really wild and remote place."

Sterling grinning, spreading his arms and hands out in a wide gesture, looking upwards. "Sure will. Big woods, way back in the interior, comparable to the amazon jungle. One way in and only one way out. Won't even hear a vehicle at all. So dark the stars will shine like diamonds and silver. Coyotes howling, and yipping. A cool breeze blows through the night to make it comfortable, unless it blows up a rain. Should we be lucky we might even hear some mysterious haunting sounds. Believe me it will be beautiful. A most wonderful experience."

Milt asked. "What mysterious sounds."

Sterling answered, "well mysterious may not fit the descriptive, but more like crickets bull frogs, owls and the like. But they can sound mysterious though. But we'll have a safety meeting before we hike off into the dange-----um bueatiful creek bottom."

Burt asked, "like what Sterling. You know something we don't? I think somethig happened to you last week."

Sterling said. "come on Burt, I'll have to be sure ya'll have insect repellant, sting ease, aspirn or other allergy medicine. Make one last check on the scout's first aid kits. making sure each one is properly prepared, with a couple of extra tee shirts. A box or two of strike on anything matches, a spare flash light. It is standard protocol. Remember at the chicken plant and where I work now? We have to have those start up safety breifs. Shouldn't take more-n- ten minutes. Let me ask you two. Do you even know the scout motto? It is, always be prepared."

Burt with a sigh of relief said. "Aw Sterling, is that all? We instill that into those boys at every meeting. We are prepared."

Sterling glances up the road. "here comes Charlene now." As she turns into the drive shutting the Surburban down and gets out with the results of a shopping spree.

"Hi Milt, Burt, ya'll doing good? Having fun with Sterling I see. Getting ready for the big event tomorrow?

Burt, chimed in as she walks toward her husband kissing him. "Hi Charlie. Yep we are ready, and anxious. The scouts been busy getting last minute preparations done and packed up. Just brought the food and drink provisions over and tied them down on the four wheeler."

Looking at Milt, "Milt, what is Ann going to do tomorrow night? Burt what about Janie? They can come over here for a while. Why we'd even go out to dinner. See who we can russel up somewhere. A ladies night out. I'm quite sure we could raise some eye brows and maybe even get talked about. We'd have a good time while ya'll are out battling."

Burt expressing a little uneasiness in his face. "We---l-l where are ya'll planning on going? I'm quite sure Jaine would be up to it."

Charlene said with a slight grin and licking her lips. "Now Burt you know bett------"

Sterling interrupting laughing, at Burt, then turns to Milt with a wondering expression. "Aw *m-a-n*, Burt you and Milt both know better than to ask that. It's a woman thang. And that means a mind thang, plus another thang."

Charlene said, "Alright Sterling," smiling at em, while Burt and Milt, glance at each other. She turns toward the house. "Honey I got your favorite Chinese dish, and mine. I'll be getting it heated up while you make final plans. I got us a movie to watch, The Great American Outdoors."

Burt said, "Milton, we need to be going. Got a get up early in the morning. Hey Charlene, we'll see you at the scout hut around 9:30 tomorrow morning. I'll tell Janie to call. She'll probably will call later this evening."

Milt said, "I'll tell Ann, knowing her, she will be game for something too. Ya'll have a good evening and we'll see you tomorrow. Are you sure they will be okay if they go out tomorrow night?" As Burt fires his green Dodge power wagen up.

Sterling walks to the passenger window looking at Milt. "Milt, those women will be all right. They won't get into any more trouble than we could. Charlene won't let em look at a Elvis much less touch em. Now ya'll go home and get some rest. Don't worry about those women." Burt backs out into the road, as Sterling stands watching them and waving. Well go in and get the movie set up and have a dish of almond duck.

Charlene said, "hi, honey, I love you so much, I had a good day out, and I'm hungry." She kisses him as they walk into the living room pulls the tv trays up to the sofa as they sat down. Sterling gets the movie on. After a few laughs through out the movie it ends.

"Ah it got done before the news and weather comes on."

"Honey I know you enjoyed the movie as much as I did. I'm a little tired and heading toward the bed room. Set the clock for when ever you leave and then I'll get up and get ready. You want us out there at the camp by eleven tomorrow."

"Yes" Ring, ting ring.

"I'll get it baby, its probably for me anyway. Hello."

"Hi Charlene."

"Hi Janie, oh yes I was expecting a call."

"Charlene you was wanting me and Ann to come over, and we'll go for a ladies, sexy." Janie looking at Burt almost laughing, "night out."

"Sure do, you game? I'm going out in my little black dress and stockings. with heels on my red shoes."

"Oh, yes I'm getting my little black dress out too. time to wear it again. With thigh highs and garter belt to hold em up and high heeled black shoes" She begins laughing as Burt chokes on his glass of tea.

"Janie give some comfort to your husband, that he'll be allright. We'll be back home before they will. Just bring Ann over with you around five tomorrow evening. Well actually any time of the day. The kids will be out playing and being chased by wild creatures. We'll chase some wild ones ourselves.

"All right, Ann and I will be right on over sometime tomorrow. Good night." Charlene could hear Burt's cry of concern when she hung the phone up laughing. "All right, Sterling honey I'm off to the bed room. What time are you getting up in the morning?"

"About five so I can have time for my coffee and prayer and God's word. Around six thirty I'll get the provisions checked and then head out to the creek. I'll meet you and the scouts at the deer hunting camp around eleven."

"I'll get up with you. I want to be at the scout cabin before they arrive, and have orange juice, and coffee made. I'll get a few dozen donuts for evey one to snack on as they arrive. Good night I love you."

"Good night I love you too. I'll be on after the news and weather." Sterling is waking, a few minutes before the alarm buzzes. He reaches over turns it off, while sitting on the edge of the bed rubbing his eyes. Then he turns to Charlene, reaching over rubbing and shaking on her shoulder. "Wake up, its time to get started."

"Already."

'Yep, I'll get the coffee brewing." He gets up staggering to the bath room. Then looks in the mirror and washes his face. Then wanders back into the kitchen and starts the coffee. Then sits down at the table.

Charlene comes through on her way to the bathroom. Coming back looking at Sterling. "Good morning, ain't you a site right now."

"Good morning, "Sleepy head."

"Coffee sure smells good. be back in a minute."

When it is brewed Sterling walks to the brewer and pours two cups, returning to the table. "Charlene, I have you a cup of coffee here."

"I'll be there in a minute honey." Sterling opens his Bible to continue reading from the previous day. While studying the chapter, Charlene comes back sitting down. "Thank you honey." After their prayer Bible study. "You know Sterling that thought does open my mind about forgiveness. And should we fall back in sin, which would be the same as falling from Grace or losing Salvation then there is no remedy for that situation. And if Jesus can't keep us clean then nothing will. So now I see that since we are forgiven then we should be thankful we can live a forgiven and free life. And you know honey, I've been a music minister in a couple of churches, and now this one. That also means to me that I should know the Bible as well as anyone. In fact we all should. But I am responsible in the ministry to show and be able to share it with anyone. And always try to instill that into the choir members, to sing as best they can from their hearts in worship of the King."

"Yep instead of continually asking for forgiveness, we should actually praise God that in Jesus Christ we are forgiven, forever."

"Hey Sterling how about some breakfast, before heading out with the supplies. I'll make a coulpe of egg and bacon bisquits. Won't take long. While the busquits are baking I'll get dressed, then primp a little before going to the hut." She leans over the table for a kiss, then gets the oven turned on and places the bisquits on a buttered pan then into the oven. Dissappearing into the bed room to get dressed, Sterling pours himself another cup of coffee, and sets down at the table. A few minutes later Charlene returns in a pair of jeans paired with a light blue western blouse. Fluffing her hair out. Then puts a few slices of bacon in the skillet, and mixes the eggs in a bowl. Sterling just sits there staring at her. *Wow, what a lady.* Charlene finishes the breakfast and puts the platter of three bacon egg and cheese bisquits on the table. She takes his cup, returns with a fresh cup of coffee.

"This sure is good, baby. I appreciate you cooking. I'm about to head out to the creek. I'll meet ya'll at the deer camp later. Hey need a few dollars for the donuts and juice or coffee?"

"I got it honey, its something I want to do for them. I'll make a couple of wise remarks about this being a good bye meal or last meal. Plus aggravate Milt and Burt about our ladies night out. Show'em how we can dress."

"Look baby don't cause them to change their minds. I have big plans. They'll encounter the escaped from a circus Lion. Then later tonight they'll hear the swamp gnat, and then be attacked by Indians. Tomorrow morning they'll be scalped. Believe me they won't come back the way they went."

"Honey don't scare em too bad."

CHAPTER 4

ATTACK, ATTACK

"Aw, whats a camping trip with out scome excitment? When they return they'll have a story to tell, if their parents keep them. I need to be heading on out. I'll see ya'll later at the deer camp." Hugging and kissing. "I love you."

"I love you too, be careful. What did you mean if their parents keep them." Now Sterling, don't let those younguns put that stuff on themselves."

"Aw, they'll be okay. Got to be heading out. See ya'll at the camp after while." Sterling walks out the door to his pickup. Pulls straight out his drive and heads west. Getting out of town, and onto the country county roads, the sun's rays lights up the landscape in a warm soft glow. He knows this is a great day for a camping excursion. The radio disc jockey is playing some good country music that fits the mood or occassion of this day. With the likes of Dave and Sugar," Queen of the silver dollar. followed by Knock three times on the celing by Tony Orlando and Dawn. The music just makes the trip much more pleasurable. Getting closer to the camp, he starts laying out plans to get away from the group, so he can get to his sound system, and lay in ambush to turn it on. Frist things first as he pulls into the deer camp property and drives down the road to the creek bottom. He stops at a dirt road leading through cutover harvested timber, and then into the remaining tember along the creek. He unloads the atv and brings it to life with a push of a button. He slowly drives into the forest and out to his right is a tall, long and wide bank, that resembles a indian buriual mound. He stops and walks out to it and sets the equipment up about half way up the side. This will be where it happens. The lion is in the woods, just waiting to growl. He returns to the atv and follows the road to where it ends on the sandbar. He makes the campsite close to the middle of the sadbar. Ah, there is a big sweet gum tree, I'll place my tent right there in it's shade. When he finishes pitching his tent, looking at his watch, well its time to head back to the meeting place. He reaches into a ice chest grabbing a coke, and rides back to the pickup and loads the atv back on the trailer, then drives back to the camp house. No one has arrived yet. I'm sure they are coming. He sits down on the door step of the camp house, drinking the coke.

A few minutes passes when he hears a vehicle approaching, and looks down the small one track black top road, to see Charlene as she turns into the drive. Sterling walks to her as she lets down her window. "Hi! Daniel Boone." Smiling at Sterling. "You have a brave company of troops to lead on this expedition. I hope they are up to the challenge."

The pack of young boys excitedly exits the Surburban putting on their back packs. Sterling glances at Burt, making sure he hears his answer. "I think they are. I'll have to lead them by that Indian burial mound. Got permission from the spirit cheif, if they'll be quiet. So hope no one gets scalped."

Burts eyes pop open and ears comes to attention. "What Sterling! Is that the danger you are going to warn us of?"

Sterling with a slight grin, said. "No. But it could be a concern, if we aren't quiet when we pass by it. Don't want to disturb the restful. Now, every one packed up and ready to march?"

A loud *"Yes."* Erupts from the troops. Charlene takes a long slurp through the straw emptying the cold drink from the cup while letting her window up.

While it is closing Sterling shouts, "good by hun, be back around eleven tomorrow morning."

Then she lets down the window again. With a laugh she commands. "Oh I almost forgot. Sterling come here. Give me your keys until I return tomorrow. So no one can demand you take them home tonight. Plus Milt and Burt won't be able to get home and try to track us three senoritas down. Ya'll ought a see our outfits. We gonna turn heads after while." Why we might get to sit by camp fires too." Taking another loud slurp, glancing at Milt and Burt. "They need to understand what preparedness really is. No one gets back until I return."

Sterling reaches into his pocket and acts as if he hands her the keys. "They really think I am giving my keys up. Thats a good one."

"Okay, I'm gone. See ya'll tomorrow. I love you, be careful. Can't wait to see what is left of this troop. Good bye." Then she speeds off into the distance as Sterling stands there watching until she is around the curve and out of sight. 'Man, I love that lil woman.'

Returning to the troop Milt ask. "Just what did she mean by that? I just can't believe you gave her your keys. What if some one gets snake bit, or happens to get sick? How are we supposed to get emergency medical care?

Sterling answers, "Milt the sout motto is always be prepared isn't it? So if any one should get bit by a snake, I'll strike up a small fire. Then pull out my nine inch bowie skinning knife hold it over the flames until all the germs are cooked and dead. Then I can cut into the bite from fang hole to fang hole and suck the venom out. If I have to cut deep and long, depending on the size of the snake and how deep he penetrated the arm or leg. The hot blade should cortorize the wound. Hopefully would be arm or leg area. I'll open my first aid kit and get the barbless fish hook stringed up with cat whiskers. Caught a stray cat last night and plucked out a few long whiskers. I even have some pulled bullets from some of my twenty two ammo. They are hard to pull from the case with the teeth. So that way I can just get a bullet and have the victim to bite down on it while I do field surgery. Its what I call field css. It is short for cut suck and sow. Seems I'm a better scout that ya'll are. Always prepared. Okay any more questions?"

Burt said "yes. Whatabout that Indian mound? You haven't said anything about Indians and their ghosts."

Sterling said. "Well Burt, you know Indians, they consider their burial grounds sacred and no one is allowed on them without proper permission. Haven't yall watched the Cartwrights, Roy Rogers, and other westerns? Oh well I wouldn't be scared of any ghosts. Probably don't exisits any way. Just immagination. Now ya'll line up. Milt you behind me and Burt bring up the rear. Oh ha, ha, ha, almost forgot to fore warn about other possible encounters." Clapping his hands together looking at the troopers. I think I should remind ya'lll about the Lion, that escaped from the circus a couple of years ago. The authorities could not locate him in this swamp. When the circus moved on then search efforts ceased. I do know he is in this area of the county. I've encountered him a time or two and sometimes late in the afternoons when I am down on the creek fishing, even hunting I can hear his roar, that reverbrates throughout this place. When it subsides, there is an eery quitness for several long minutes. But I wouldn't worry too much about getting caught and eaten."

Scout George said. "Every one who wants to hike back home raise your hands." Instantly Milt and Burt along with scout Albert raises their hands. The remaining five follows suit.

Sterling said. "Aw comeon ya'll, its futher to hike home than it is down to the creek. Then ya'll can cool off while playng and swimming. We need to strike out ahead. Just listen to me and you'll be safe and have the most wonderful experience. Any way that Lion won't eat any one. Humans aren't on his diet list. Got plenty of other creatures to munch on. squirrels, rabbits, rats, and the like. Might be one reason I haven't encountered many snakes lately. In fact that old tom cat has gotten so big and strong on that diet, he can stalk around a water hole or even along the creek and snatch ducks and other water fowl right out of the air as they try to lift off in escape. That main has gotten so thick and tough its like a iron curtian around his body. Oh I'll know if we should get close to em. That wild cat smell will be strong. Just have to ease along with caution and not make any sudden moves to run."

Scout albert asked in a low nervous voice. "But what if he does get after us. What should we do?"

Sterling answering, while pushing his straw stethson up, holding his twelve guage Remington eleven eighty seven semi-auto shotgun over his shoulders. Then resting his right hand on the Ruger .22 mag revolver resting in his holster. Well neither of these guns will be effective against a charge. It'll be whoever can run the fastest. And I think I can run faster than any of ya'll."

Tears flowing down his eyes scout George remarked. "I wished I hadn't come out here now. If my mommy knew this she would come and get me. I don't want to get caught by a ghost or be eaten."

Sterling assured him. "come on scout George grow up a little. Be a little brave scout. I promise to take care of ya'll. Then pulling out the bottle of repellant, and opening the it. "Okay now every one is required to put a coating of this on. It will offer great protection from the most dreadful creature out here. And I'm the only person who knows about it. Because no one believes me. Weather ya'll believe me or not put it on or stay here by yourselves. No shelter, no food, no nothing until tomorrow sometime.

Scout George takes the bottle first and begins pouring it on his arms. Sterling commands. "Hold on scout George thats a plenty. Whew, you are powerfully protected now pass it on to scout Edward, Albert and Albert to Poco, to Milt jr. on to Bob, Johnny, Robert and Roy. Roy drops it, not touching. He then pretends to rub this stuff on himself, Any left Milt and Burt gets it."

Milt asks, "Sterling what is that stuff? The more they put on, the worse it gets. Little Milt I think your momma is going to be excited and upset. We have mosquito repellent. But this stuff?"

Sterling said, "Pick that bottle up Burt, before any more is wasted." Taking his shotgun off his shoulder holding it pointed toward the ground away from every one. "Yes Milt the off is good for mosquitos, but I assure you this is not a mosquito." Not wanting to handle that bottle with the repellant smeard on it. "Hope there is enough for you two. Well I do have a spare for emergency."

Burt commented. "I just don't see why this is all of a sudden necessary. You didn't tell us about all this last night. Just what is out there waiting for us?"

Sterling said, "Aw Burt." While resting the shotgun across his bent knee. "Y'all probably wouldn't believe me if I told ya. Thats the main reason I'm having ya'll put this protection potion on. Besides ain't nothing waiting on ya'll out there any way. Well maybe one thing. That is why you're putting this on."

While rubbing the potion on Burt moned and whined. "Man this stuff stinks. It is already getting stronger by the minute."

Sterling asked. "Do ya'll want to go camping or act like a bunch of scardy cats?"

The troopers shouted in unison. "Lets go camping."

"Sterling said. "okay get this repellant rub on and into your skin. Mainly arms and neck. The most exposed areas of your body. But wouldn't hurt to rub a little on your chest and stomach. And while you're at it with those shorts on rub those legs too. Lets get protected all over."

Burt swaying his arms out and holding them up starts coughing whinning. "Powerful is not the word for this stuff."

Milt replied. "I-I-II may not be allowed back home. I wonder what Ann is is doing with Janie and Charlene."

Sterling is walking up and down the formed line while the boys are rubbing themselves inspecting their coatings. Burt slips to the front of the line to Milton whispering. "Milt I should've known better than to agree with ya'll about this character taking us out here in danger. Oh I know there is something just looming out there, waiting for us. He Charlie is a pair of a kind. Just right for each other. They are a magnet for danger. Plus like him with us out here, so Ann and Janie are with her. Plus if I'm correct he was attacked by some swamp creature last week."

Milt exclaimed, with widening eyes and fright on his face. *"What! Sterling! Something happened last week you're not telling us about?"*

Sterling replied with a slight grin. "Aw Milt, it was nothing really. Didn't even get a scratch." Sterling looking at the troopers clapping his hands. "Every one soaked in repellant and ready to march?"

Socut Robert asked. "Mister Sterling, aren't you going to tell us why we have to have this on us, before we march off?"

Sterling said in a laughing voice. "Oh ha, ha, ha." Begins his walk up and down the line again. "Might ought to, bout forgot. Yep, ya'll might have to replenish it around dark."

Burt interrupts. "I don't think this will need to be renforced. This stuff is getting stronger by the minute. I know now I'll never be allowed at home. Should've just took my chances of not encountering this thing or maybe just try swatting it off."

Sterling pulling his straw custom fitted stethson down. "ha, aha, h------Not this creature Burt. Good thing though, there aren't but only two or three in existence."

Scout Bob asked. "What does this thing look like? I'm getting scared."

Milt interrupted. "You're scared? I think this whole troop is scared. Don't know what lies ahead."

Sterling getting control said. "Milt they aren't scared, just excited. Whats a camping trip without some excitement? Ya'll will come away with a story. Well okay, ya'll listen up, one time through is all I'm telling. This creature is what I call at the moment the swamp gnat. He looks like a regular ole gnat but several thousand times bigger." While extending his arms. "However." With widening eyes, looking up and down the line. "His body is about eight to ten feet round, solid black, with sprounts of nasty hair growing, like weeds in a wet muddy bog. Wing span of around fourteen to sixteen feet. Big black boulbous head with a hyperdemic needle like snout. Three rows of legs with three toes on each leg. Now unlike the Swamp Lion he preys on anything with blood veins. Whe he gets those wings flapping and becomes airborne, sounds like a squadron of B-25 bombers on a mission. Which usually he is."

Burt interrupts. "Think maybe we could stay in this camp house?"

Scout Albert said. "I think that would be a good idea. Mister Sterling, reckon you could go down to the creek and bring our supplies back?"

Sterling answered. "Nope sure can't, remember Charlene had to have my keys atv included. Any way I thought ya'll wanted to learn about being brave, in the wildernesss and prepared so ya'll can receive your camping badge. Besides those large wood rats and snakes hiding from that escaped lion might be in there. They'd have a feast for sure. Thats it get those packs back on. Milt you and Burt ok? Looks like ya'll are about to pass out. Looks like ya'll may have seen a ghost.

Now back to the swamp gnat, his legs is what to be wary of. Stay out from under them if he attacks. He swoops down on ya from high in the sky. Leveling off in his power dive he grabbs your back and neck with those toes, for a secure grip and flies you to the creek and lands on the sandbar. He then takes three toes from another leg to clamp your mouth and nostrils together, so you won't reek out in seveir pain when he burries that hypodermic needle like snout deep into your juglar vein and sucks all your blood out in in one slurp. And most of ya'll wouldn't even be one good slurp. Remember how Charlene was slurping on her straw, sucking her drink out of the cup? So on another note too, right now ain't no time to wonder what those three women are doing. Might be considering garnering new husbands."

Burt said in a quavering voice. "I-I-I-II would rather be with mine right now. We're out here enduring scent, summer heat that makes it worse, an--an--and about to bec---com--me a me-mea-meal. And Sterling is right, our wives may be out looking for other men. Sterling does Charlee know something we don't?"

Sterling replied. "Not that I know of. Maybe it is womens tution, who knows."

Scout Johnny raised his hand. Sterling acknowledges. "Yes scout Johnny."

Scout Johnny asked trying to be brave and voiceful. "Mister Sterling, are you sure this thing exists? I wonder if you're just trying to scare us."

Scout Roy said. "Yea, I think you're tryig to scare us."

Sterling acting as if he is angry at the statement. "All right, *attention!* Ya'll listen really good. I'm going to tell ya'll what happened last week." While walking up and down the line of troops. Last week I was going fishing. I leisurely walked down that path we are about to embark on. I heard him go into a dive. Instantly I knew I was under attack. I had forgot my repellant. I took a bounding dive forward to the ground, rolling to the side out from under em, hoping he would miss. During the tumble, I drew my eight inch Damacus steel bowie knife. When he leveled off and trying to adjust his grab. I made a swath at him cutting a leg as he tried to get back up above me. He reeked out in pain as blood spurted onto the ground splattering a little on me. He climbed into the blue yonder, to make another attempt on me."

The whole troop gasps putting their hands over their mouths. Scout Roy Exclaimed. *"Wow!* Mister Sterling, how'd you get away?"

"Thats what I'm about to tell ya'll." Stepping toward Burt at the rear, then glancing back down the line, all eyes on him. He turns back down the line. "This is why you don't want to forget the repellant. this rascal is determined to get into the veins of any thing that has them. As the attack heightened I heard him revving up those wings as he climbed into the wild blue yonder. Wings glistening in the sun as he looped over head. I looked toward the creek making a mental path straight to it. Then I looked back to get locked in on his position. Breathing hard and crouched down I checked my only path to the creek. As he desended out of the loop, coming after me, I broke into a mad dash straight foward. Crashing, running as fast as I could through briar patches, thorn bushes and thickets. Staying as low as possible. He was close behind zig zagging back and forth dodging limbs. Plus I was ripping those briar barbs and thorns off so fast that they must've been like bullets from a machine gun buzzing back towards him. after he couldn't take any more he climbed higher. When I ran into the open forest I knew I was close to the creek. Standing by a large oak trying to make myself as small as I could while searching the sky, and listening. Not hearing anything I slipped along through the trees, emeging to a small clearing on a cliff of the creek. Making one last search into the sky I heard him coming in low to my right. Only one thing to do, break out across the clearing diving off the twenty foot cliff to the creek below. Going off the edge I broke the surface of the creek as he leveled off snatching at me ripping the back out of my tee shirt. As he gained altitude I surfaced the water searching for a hollow weed on the bank. Just barely found one breaking it off I dived back under water. I swam down creek to a log jam hoping there wouldn't be a snake any where around. Just about out of air I eased the weed out of the water so I could breathe. Boy that was a relief. Then after about an hour of hovering over the water, because he knew I was there somewhere, he began poking the water with that long snout. I saw only his shadow easing down the creek toward my position. Before I could swim to another location that snout passed beside me, missing by a hair. When he pulled back up to make another stab I darted under the log jam. just barely get the tip of my nose above water, so I could breath. For the next couple of hours he flew up and down that part of the creek jabbing for me. So I guess he got tired or figured I got out of the creek without him noticing, he flew off into the direction of where we came from. I held my position for another hour or so making sure he was gone. When I emerged from the creek I looked like a shrivled prune."

Milt asked, "isn't there somewhere else we could camp, or a safer route to get to our camp site?"

Still acting a little disgruntled, Sterling answered. "Look, Milt we done been here just about too long. It is time to march on."

Scout Robert raises his hand. "Mister Sterling have you found any victims of the gnat?"

Sterling replied, with a laugh, "yep sure have." glancing up and down the line again with attention on Milt and Burt. One these swamp gnats, probably the one that attacked me, dived on one of Farmmer Goza's cows, and flew em to the creek. I discovered the cow one day while fishing. Upon inspecting the carcass, it was just as I figured. That swamp gnat had a meal, burried his snout, into the juglar vein and sucked the blood out so hard it pulled the cow's hide up tight against his bone structer."

Burt interrupting as the scouts take in a gasping breath, in unison *"gosh!"*

Burt said in a high pitched voice. *"Thatsit!* I'm not---- going downinthat-- swamp."

The troops begins snuffling and crying, *"we want a go home."*

Sterling using his comforting voice said. "Hold on a minutenow. Ya'll wanted to go camping. Ya'll calm down a second. The way ya'll smell right now will highly diminish an encounter with any thing in the swamp. mosquitos, gnats, and other insects that compete for your veins. So an attack from this creature probably won't happen. He can't get past the scent protection of the repellant."

Milt said, "now I can see and smell why any thing within scent range would'nt come near us."

Sterling renforcing his statement said. "Thats right Milt. The scent of the repellant is lifting off ya'll and already floating down towards the swamp. Every creature may vacate the premis. Probably already on the other side of the creek."

Burt said, "Good, thats just what we want."

Sterling ordering, "every one get lined up again, we are moving out. F-O-W-A-R-D M-A-R-C-H. Hup, o-n-e, two, three, four, sound off."

The troops sounded off to their marching as they began. But then quieted down as the summer heat rose as they marched down the first hill. "Okay Milt when we get out of the hills and into the swamp we'll stop for a fifteen minute rest. I'll give futher instructions there. *Alright troops! lets step it up, like renforcements going to replace other troops in combat."*

Milt asked, "What do you mean?"

Sterling answered. "While ya'll are resting, I'll go into the swamp ahead and scout for posible danger. It's just a safety precaution."

Milt trying to keep up a conversation asked. "That shotgun, what kind is it? Reckon it can ward off either of those creatures?"

"It is a Remington 11-87 semi auto shotgun. It'll handle any two and three quarter inch shot shells and the powerful three inch loads. The side arm I have on is a Ruger single six convertable twenty two. Convertable means it'll take both a twenty two long rifle cylinder and the longer magnum cylinder." He then pulls the revolver out of the holster. "See Milt, I have the powerful twenty two Winchester magnum. It s loaded with Winchester forty grain full metal case ammo. And I can shoot the stripes off of pole cats at a hundred and fifty yards. And bust coyotes hides at little over a hundred with a load of Remington, three inch number five shot. So stop worrying and enjoy the hike." About forty five minutes later a hot tired sweaty, and smelly company of troops arrive at the turn site. He orders *"company--- halt. Drop your packs and take a fifteen minute break. Take a few sips of water."*

While they are getting their packs off Burt mumbles while wheezing and gasping for breath. "Its about time we stop for a break. How much farther do we have to go?"

Sterling, not even breathing hard answers. "Not far now. Only a couple of hundred yards down this trail, and we'll be on the creek."

Scout Albert breathing a little hard said *"Whew!"* Wiping his forehead, "all this sweating really has this stuff in force."

Scout Roy said, "you can say that again. Momma and Daddy will probably put me up for adoption."

Sterling taking control of the complaints said forceful. "All right listen up. In about fifteen or twenty minutes, I want ya'll to move down the trail. Milt, you will be in charge for now. The trail leads straight to the creek. At that point it'll take a ninety degree turn to the left. It'll drop down a slight hill. leading to the sandbar and camp site. If I haven't met back up with ya'll just stop there and wait for me."

"Burt, scared ask, "And where are you going?"

Sterling staring him down, answering. "Aw come on Burt. You know I have to go out and scout that area, to ensure your safety. Would you like to do this?"

Burt mumbled weakly, "Noo-ooo-oo."

Sterling ordered. "Then you bring up the rear and we'll all get out to the camp site safely. See ya'll later." Sterling walks off into the cutover and stops for a minute listening.

Burt looking at Milt. "Milton, why just why did you have to go out and find Daniel Boone, Davey Crockett, and Indianna Jones rolled up into one to lead us off into this wilderness? Did you see him give Charlie his pickup keys? We have no way to get home, except to walk. Right now we don't know how far home is from here. All we have is an idiot that says you are here. I haven't heard one vehicle on a road since we left."

Then Sterling returned back to the party, grinning, "Oh I just about to forget to explaine necessary procedures in case an attack happens." He reaches into a jeans pocket pulling out plastic drinking straws, and hands them to each individual. "If that swamp gnat tries to over power the repellant and gets after ya'll, here is what to do. Rush straight out to the creek as fast as you can. Then get under water. Use these straws to breath through until I can get that rascal off ya'll. These straws will be easier to breath through than a hollow weed. Here take two or three apeice. That giant gnat spots a straw sricking out of the water, he will pinch the straw shut. I guarantee you will rise to the surface quickly. Be an easy slurp then. If that should happen just release that straw and, and swim quickly staying under water, to another location, and, put up your other straw. Now if that lion should roar, he has smelled ya'll or he is on the prowl. Just get behind a large tree or lay flat on your stomach behing a log, until he passes by. Don't try to out run em. You are caught should you try."

Milton mumbling, scared, tears begin to well up in his eyes. "My-m-m-my- m-y Gosh! What ever persuaded us to want to come out in a place like this to camp. Especially like the scout reservation."

Scout Albert crying wiping his eyes. "Mister Sterling sir, Ple-ple-please don- don- don't leave us a- a-alone out here."

Sterling looking into his sad eyes, encouraged him. "don't worry little Albert. I'm just going out there to make sure there is no danger. Should it be I'll get rid of it. I'll see ya'll later. "Then he turns and dissappears into the swamp.

Burt said, "who is in favor of trying to get outta here?"

Scout Roy said, "II think we should move on down this trail. Any way, bad as we smell we have this whole swamp to ourselves."

Milt said, "well he left me in charge so we'll move slowly and carefully down the trail. Keep your eyes open. Lets get our packs on and move out."

The troop stands and stretches then dons, their packs. Burt working his arms through the straps then with a hump and half jump mumbles as he takes his first couple of steps. "*Gosh!* I can't believe we are actually doing this. I'll be glad when I get back home. *Whew!* This stuff stinks. Just hope Janie will let me come back home. *Whew!*" As the pack marches down the trail Burt pauses for a moment wiping sweat from his forehead with his floppy hat then stares back in the direction from where he came. Listening for any sounds that may cause concern. A feeling of loneliness comes over him as he looks back for the party and no one is in sight. Then just catching a glimpse of movement through the trees in the direction of the troops, he breaks out into a trot to catch up.

Scout Johnny said, "I think he is shooting us a mouth full of balonga. He's probably out there right now laughing at us. I'll be glad when we get to the creek and set up camp. Then dive into the creek and try to cut some of this stinking stuff." hau, hau, hau, hauk, hauk, A-choo, a-choo. Sterling sitting by his sound system listens to their wheezing, sneezing, and coughing, just before he spots movement on the trail. As they march into a spot where he can see them, he turns on the tape player. Gr--a-a-a-w--o-l, gro-oo-oow-l.

Milt yells, 'sw-s-sw-s-w-swam-swamp gn-gn-gnat run, run for the creek. Burt faints on the spot, a couple of scouts dives behind a big log. Sterling notices a spray of sand upwards of twelve feet, marking the spot where Milt and a couple of scouts hit the sandbar and a spray of water when they splashed into the creek. Sterling points his shotgun downward on a forty five degree angle, pulling the trigger. *Poooooooow-poooooooooow-poooooooooow,* reverbrating through the forest, then a quietness. He walks briskly to the road where Burt lies and the scouts hunkered down by a log and a couple of big oak trees. Gathering them up as they are shouting and hollering, then rushes to the creek. Milt, Milt jr., Johnny, Poco, and Albert standing in knee deep water trembling while holding straws up.

He orders, "Ya'll come on out of the creek. Why did ya'll run to the creek. It was the lion not the swamp gnat. Could've had ya'll for dinner. Come on lets get to the camp site. Dragging a small log close to the camp site. Ya'll just sit right here, while I get Burt." He grabs a bucket, walks down to the creek. He dips the bucket under water then lifts it up. The bucket about half filled he half walks and half runs to the road where Burt is still laying. Walking to him Sterling pours the water. Splash, as it rolls over Burt, hitting the ground dry dirt becomes mud splashing up on Burt.

He jumps up shaking his head hau hu hauk ha, ha ahuk trying to catch his breath breaks into a run screaming. "Ru-ru-ru-run fo-fo-for runforthe creek."

Sterling chasng him down, "Burt, Burt, Burt, calm down every thing is alright now. It was the lion stalking around the mound. Almost trotted right into me. May have been stalking me. When he roared I fired on em."

"Tha-tha-that gun sounded like a cannon going off. I-I-I'm sure you mus-mus-must have bag-bag-bagg-ed em."

"Nope, just burned him enough to change his mind. He broke out across the creek, heading futher into the woods. Thats it calm down calm down. You're safe now, lets head on to the camp, where every one else is. We'll gather some fire wood for camp, and get ye tents up."

"We-we-wel-well I -I-I jus-jus-just hop-hop-hop-e nothing els-els-els-else hap-hap-happ-ens. Thi-thi-this a-a-a-tta-attack jus-jus-jus-just too-too-took ten-ten-ten years of-off- my-my-my lif-life."

"Aw you'll be okay. Come on lets get to camp." Burt staggers into camp trailing a few steps. Sterling orders. "Milt you and a couple of scouts get that big long log over there and drag it up here. Lay it down across this way. You other scouts start gathering fire wood." Milt and his three, scouts drags the log up and drops it as each one groans and moams about how heavy it was.

"That is not where it needs to be. Slide it on over this way a couple of feet." That done and fire wood gathered up for an extended campout. "Attention Sterling ordered. "Ya'll know what is next on the to do list right?"

Scout Roy raised his hand. Sterling acknowledged, "Yes scout Roy?"

Scout Roy said. "Next thing is we set our tents up."

Sterling, welcomed his answer. "Yes scout Roy the tents has to be set up properly before any one can go to the creek. So lets do it." While they unpack their tents Sterling builds up the fire place. Then looking at the scouts. "Okay I want ya'll to put your tents up in a circle around this fire place. About ten feet away. We need a fifteen foot space between each tent." Then pointing back toward the trail they came in on. "Burt go about three quarters of the distance between the scouts camp to the trail and set your tent up."

Burt began mumbling, "but-but-but, why way over there?"

Sterling ordered. "Just listen to me it is important. Now Milt take your tent and get down there close to the creek."

Milt said, "who me?"

Sterling said, "yes you, who else. Now ya'll get em set up and then report back." About fifteen minutes they came back. "Looking at their set up. Sure you have it done sturdy and correctly?" They both nodded yes. "Alright now check and make sure these scouts are setting up correctly."

Sterling, Milt and Burt are walking around them watching. "Well Milt, Burt think they are doing a job worth an A plus in the scout manuel?"

Milt glances at Burt and Milt said, "yes."

Sterling asked as they stood around the fire site. "Ya'll have your tents set up good-n-tight?"

They answered, "yes sir."

Sterling ordered. "Alright lets get the fire wood stacked up and ready to start and then ya'll will be excused to paly, swim, or fish in the creek."

Scout Edward raised his hand. Sterling acknowledges. "Mr. Sterling, why did you have us to set the tents up in a circle around the camp fire? And Mr. Milt's and Mr. Burts out and away from us?"

Sterling answered. "Well thats a pretty good question, but every one of ya'll should know. Pushing his stethson up leaning foward on a bent knee, and wiping his forehead. Well when Milt, Johnny, Poco and Albert shot through the woods screaming and hollering, it may have disturbed those ghost Indians up on their mound. So there may be a reaction later. Hope not. But for safety we are encircled. With my tent right back here towards the back of camp I can watch over ya'll. In the case with Milt and Burt. See they are on the outskirts too. So that way if those Indians decide to try something they would be the first to know and send out their warning signal. First screaming and then hollering from a scalping. That way we'll know to get behind this log for protection from flying arrows and bullets. Ain't ya'll ever watched any westerns on television? Wagon Train, especially, they always park in a circle. Man talking about protection. Even though a couple of them do get hit by an arrow. But most of the time they survive.

And also according to the one who screams or hollers first I'll know which direction to start shooting first. Since we are in a circle they'll have charge around us."

Scout Edward said. "Oh yea, I see now, this is a great set up. Just like in a real western." With eyes widening fear began to come on him. "Mr. Sterling. They going to be shooting real bows and arrows, and guns at us?"

"Sterling answered while glancing at Milt and Burt with dropped jaws, and popping eyes. "Sure will. Ain't never heard of an attack without weapons. Yep they could be after our scalps."

Burt said. "Sterling, thats why you want us out there alone?"

Sterling answered. "Yep", while pulling down his stethson. Now what you are allowed to do here. Ya'll can take a supply of fire wood and build a comfort fire for the long nite ahead. Like a night light at home. Keep both ears open when you lay down and sleep with one eye open."

Burt remarked. "I-I-I-I doubt I'll ge-ge-get any sl-sl-sle-sle-ep tonight."

Milt said, "I don't think any of us will get much sleep tonight."

Burt said, "We done got out here and gonna be on the skinning rack. No wonder Charlie got Janie and Ann to go out with her. Some other cowboys will take their minds off us. They'll never look for us."

Sterling said, "Aw Burt I wouldn't think like that too much. Heck we got more -n-that to keep us occupied other than those three wido-uh-uh pretty women. Shoot! Times a wasting. Troop dismissed. You are free to get in the creek. I'll be right up here watching every thing and listening. I'll signal with a owl call and wave this white rag as a signal to report back to camp and get ready for the cook out. You're free to go.

Calming down a little as they stagger across the loose white sand bar to the creek. Burt with his rod and lure box in hand. "Milt I'm going right up there to that point where the sand bar points into the creek. Looks like a good spot to start fishing. I'll work that tree top and then move on to the logs."

"Yea, Burt I think maybe its going to be enjoyable now. I just hope Sterling run that lion off. Man he had a bad growl."

"Yes, even double growled. And evidently Sterling knows what he is talking about. Haven't heard anything that might even suggest an aireal attack from that swamp gnat."

"Well let me get back to those kids. If you hear even the slightest sound get back here quick. Hope you land a bigun. good luck."

"Thanks lil buddy. Already I'm hungry. can almost smell those hotdogs smoking over the fire."

"Yep and those marshmallows. We'll make a lot of smores. Okay see ya later. Keep the camp in sight now. Wonder what those wives are really going to be up too."

While the troops are splashing and playing in the creek, Sterling sets up his personal table and a couple of lawn chairs around it. He walks over to the ice chest and gets a coke. Returns to his table and sits down. Pop splish crack, as he opens the coke and takes a sip. Man this is good on a hot afternoon as this. I got the best spot right here off to the side of the main camp under this big sweetgum tree. Won't be as hot tonight as those boys tents will be.

As the afternoon changes to evening, the scouts all shrivled up begans the return to camp. Sterling is milling about along the rock bar searching for special rocks, enjoying the time. He looks up and right down the middle of the creek the sun appears to be setting in it. It's softer orange rays turn the gently flowing water to a soft orange color. Bull frogs began their croacking, crickets chirping as the sun drops rapidly in the west. The fresh sent of the creek wraffles on a slight southwestern breeze, announcing the message of night fall. He returns to camp. The boys and Milt are standing around the fire location rubbing their hands on their soaked, dripping shorts in anticipation of a warming fire.

Milt suggest. "Sterling lets get the fire started. We are hungry."

Burt said. "You are right about that out here on this creek and fishing has me just about starving."

Sterling ordered. "All right first things first. *Whew!* Yall are smelling something powerful now. First get away from the fire place, you're getting it wet. Go to your tents and get dried and uniforms back on. Be out here in about ten minutes. Sterling returns to his table and sits down. Burt returns from his tent walks over and sits down with Sterling. Sterling is staring out into the distance back toward the road.

Burt ask, "Sterling what is it? What are you staring at?"

Milt walks up and sits down in the other chair. "What is it?"

Sterling answeres *"sh-sh-sh.* Be quiet before those boys come out."

Milt wishpering ask, "What is it Sterling? I don't hear any thing."

Burt said, "Me either."

Sterling raises his hand. "I been hearing that sound all afternoon. Just hoping that wasn't what I was hearing. I'm pretty sure it is the war drums beating."

Burt shouted out "What!" Sterling I don't hear anything. I think you could be just hearing things."

Sterling said, "Nope, I saw smoke signals about thirty minutes ago. Just be quiet Burt, you're gonna make the situation even more dangerous."

Burt said "Milt I'm going right now and move my tent into the protection circle."

Milt said. "lets go and getum. They ain't gonna get me out there by my self."

They break out into a run to their tents picking them up and running back to the camp site, placing their tents in the circle line close to Sterling's.

Milt asks. "Sterling are'nt you going to move your tent within the circle of protection?"

Sterling answers, "Nope, I'll be alright where mine is under that big sweetgum tree. Its only about thirty yards back up from the camp circle. I can see just about every thing over ya'll. Alright ya'll lets get the fire started. You scouts do it. Milt, you and Burt get the camp table set up with the buns and condiments on it. Scouts Roy and Johnny, you two go over to that hedge bush and get a dozen limber switches off it." Soon a roaring camp fire lights the camp in the twilight. While darkness settles in and the fire flickers down, the tents are a faint glow in the flames. A couple of scouts pull their hot dogs out of the fire and walks to the table and dresses it up on the bun. Then they grab a hand full of chips then sets down on the log. Another one laughs when his marshallows flame up. "Hey Milt you and Burt go and get that log behind my tent. We could use more sitting room."

When they get behind the tent they began mumbling and grumblin with each other, as they search for the log. "Darn Milt, I told you things happen to this guy. He has been listening to war drums all evening, while we were in the creek. I don't see no log."

"Lets just find that log and get it back to camp before some warrior takes us prisioners. Silver will never find us. Oh here it is. Get on the other end and lets just pick it up and get back inside the camp. Look lets just try to relax and have a good time."

"Milt just how can I. I just feel like I'm being watched right now. Some indian ready to pounce on me."

"Burt, let s just get this log and go. Ain't far. Plus think on the bright side. We need to get those younguns out into a real wilderness. They will have a story to tell when they get back home."

"Yea, Milt if we get back home. Who'd a thought Indians woulda been out here. Pick up the pace, before we get nabbed and scalped."

Mumbling, "wouldn't get much hair from you would they."

"You think that is just funny eh. You gonna loose your hair sooner than you think." Coming back into camp gasping. "Sterling, you want it right here?" As they drop it close to the one being occupied.

Sterling commanded, "nope, nope, nope. Some of you scouts roll the log to the end of this one and turn it down the other side of the fire."

The laughter and chatter continues, hot dogs turn brown and black in the fire. Some marshallows flame up. Sterling watches the scouts having fun and thinks how lucky they are to be out here. In real wild camping. Its sad that many scouts will only get to camp on a nicely manicured site. Complete with tent pad. Tame camping I call it.

He stands up, pulling his stethson lower. "Milt ya'll think the scouts are doing good towards their camping badge Requirements?"

Milt and Burt looks at each other then casts a view over the scouts, then back at each other with a agreeing concenious. Milt said. "Yes they are doing it by the book."

Sterling asks, "but it seems like something is being left out. Now just what could it be? Ya'll think about it. They aren't quite up to snuff yet."

Burt said, "Oh yea, when every one is through eating, we are supposed to sit around the camp fire, sing songs and tell some stories. And of course my favorite make smores."

Milt and Burt sits down on the log with the scouts and Sterling sets down toward the end. Milt said, "okay yall, I know we all know the words to the song, Way Down Upon the Swany River. We'll begin with that one and any one else who has a favorite we'll try to sing it too. Every one ready? A on, aone, aone atwo athree. The whole troop joins in as Sterling leans to the side for a few minutes.

They finish the song, then Burt said. "Keep up the good work, how about I came From Alabama, With A Banjo On my Knee."

Sterling slips his hand into his pocket and pulls out the long range special remote. Looks at the troops while they are into the singing. The fire flickers, casting a warm glow on their faces and dimly lit tents in the back ground. He pushes the on button to start the sound of B-25 bombers taking off in a war movie. "*Wha-zat!*" Then turns it off.

Scout George stops singing, looking at Sterling. "Wha-what, I didn't hear anything."

Scout Albert pausing, "Aw its probably nothing Grorge."

They join back in with the singing and Sterling raising the volum turning it on, then back off. He said looking around as if searching for the source of the sound. "*Wha-zat!* I know I heard something then."

Scout Elmore stops singing, looking around and upwards into a night starry sky. Asked, "Mr. Sterling, what do you think it is. Cause I heard it too."

Burt stops the singing. Stares up into the night sky, cuffing his hand on his ear, with mouth partly open. Milt and the other scouts are quiet and listening for strange sounds. Sterling calling back attention. "It probably wasn't nothing. I don't hear it any more. Go back to singing."

Milt said, "I think its time for a story. Sterling think you could tell us what happened earlier today?"

Sterling rises slowly and eases to the front of the scouts. Looking at all the faces with wide eyes focusing their attention on him. The fire flickers down to a small flame, that reveal the triangular tents. He pushes his stethson up off his forehead. He makes special eye contact with each of the party. Then he said, "it happened like this." Pointing toward the dirt road. "See when I left ya'll up there on the trail, It seemed I'd forgot to tell ya'll about that Indian burial mound. Or did I?"

Burt interrupted. "I-I-I think you did mention it in passing. said something about being quiet and not upsetting the restful."

"Oh thats right I did mention it. I even told ya'll about those spirits that guard it. See they can conjure up the whole tribe if they need to. I had secured permisson for us to pass by. But anyway." Eyes widening crouching down into a stalk, he stealthy stalked up the line of an in awe group. I slowly, silently stepped upon that mound, pausing, studying the area in front of me. In a moment that big lion pounced off a limb high in a oak tree. He was about thirty yards out. Those hungry cold yellows eyes watched me. I could all but feel the coldness from that stare. Felt pretty good considering the summer heat. Well he had been watching ya'll from his vantage point. In a angry rage he raised up on his hind legs. Lips curled revealing those long needle like cannines, and licking his lips with that rough sandpaper like tongue. That long thick mane flowing down his eight or ten foot frame. Looked like a monster. Reminded me of the once in a life time hunting trip to Africa and the one I shot at. With a big double barrled rifle. Oh ha, ha, ha, thats another story. Anyway he was also pawing the air with his large paws with the claws sticking out. *Swish, swish, swish, swish.* Instantly he dropped down and charged. I just barely got my shotgun to my hip and started firing. He ran right past me toward the creek. Thought he was after ya'll. Being in the creek like that, makes for a easy meal. I did hear him diving off into the creek and then shaking that heavy thick fur and mane, then silence. Couldn't hear nothing for all the screaming and crying from ya'll."

Scout Poco raised his hand, and Sterling acknowledged. Sir, sir, si um Mr. Sterling think you might a killed that lion?"

Sterling answering, while pulling his Stethson down over his forehead. "Nope, In the quickness of the moment all I could do was maybe fire a bit high right over em. See we've bumped into each other on occassions before. I think we recogonized each other. So far we both have survived. Actually he could've had me, however I think we are just playing cat and mouse. He knows as well as I do if one of us takes the other out then the saga ends. And neither of us wants that, so he made a fast exit across the creek."

Burt said, "sco-sco-scout, scouts lets roast a few more hot dogs and marsh mallows, and make some smores. By-by-by th-th-the way, Sterling ho-how, was hi-hi-his body sha-shape. I mean he didn't seem to be hun-hung-hungry or any anything like that di-did he?"

All eyes and ears glued on Sterling, he pushes his hat up, putting hands on hips, right knee, bending slightly. Matter of fact, when he blew past me, I saw his rib cage, probably could've counted most of his ribs." Then he punches a marsh mallow on a stick and lowers it into a dying fire.

Scout George said, "I-I-I, thought you said yo-yo-you could sho-sho-sho-shoot stri-stripes of-of-off a skunk at three hundred and twenty yards."

Sterling said, "well George, I might can do that. But look this was no skunk." Withdrawing his marsh mallow out of the fire when it flames into a ball of fire. "Somebody better throw another log on the fire. I really ain't go no reason to kill a creature such as this. It'll take the fun out of camping. I only hunt and fish for the enjoyment and do some of my part in game animal population control. Ain't never hurt the population in any game I've hunted, big or small."

Scouts Roy and Johnny, goes to the fire wood pile and brings back a couple of big chunks and lays on the fire. Soon it is perks up. Milt said, "Sterling, you mean we are stuck out here with creatures like this? And you treat um as if they are pets. It is plumb scary, that rascal could waltz right in here and get any one he chooses. If he were mind and hungry to."

Sterling chuckling and pulling his stethson down. "He won't get me I guarantee that."

Scout Albert asked. "How do you know you won't be the one he gets?"

Sterling answers, "Because I can run faster than any of ya'll." Then a panic expression evokes the whole troop.

Burt suggests, "Okay, okay, okay enough about that dreaded cat. Wel-well just a sec-second. Was it a male or female?"

Sterling getting down, staring each one in their eyes. Lifting his hat up above him, said. "He is a big male. On a good day his weight would be around seven hundred pounds. But he looked like he was down a couple hundred."

Scout Bob asked, "How do you know it was a male?"

Continuing his stare, and glancing at Burt annd Milt. "Well he had a big thick mane. Also a thick needle sharp tuft, well pile of fur on top of his head. He probably could put that head down and charge you. You would stick to that fur like velcro and lift you up on top, and tote you off to his den and have a snack."

The troops began snuffling, wiping their eyes with the back of their hands, and Burt mumbles. "*M-m-my gos-gosh!* Why did I-I-I ev-ever agree with thi-thi-this camp ou-outing."

Milt said, "You, you troops calm down. Mr. Silver is just stretching things a bit. Ya'll know that. Sterling you're getting us scared."

Sterling said, "Well! Its not my fault. It was ya'll that wanted to hear about what happened up there. Besides they're only excited. So why don't ya'll tell a story or two."

Scout Johnny tried to tell a story but just couldn't get it out from the fright inside him. No one else speaks up, Milt said. "Lets sing another song or two, then maybe some one could share a story. How about She'll be coming round that mountain when she comes."

They began to sing. Sterling is setting, in his lawn chair just inside the encampment. Trying to avoid the excess heat form more logs being thrown on the fire. He slides a hand into his pocket acquiring the remote and turns it on turning the volume up just a little, and the sound of B-25 bombers in flight. Then quickly turns it off. 'Wha-zat, listen. I know I heard something. I just know I did."

Milt said, "loo-lo-lo-look ya-ya-ya'll don-don't list-en t-t-t-to him. Hes ly-ly-lying." Sterling then turns it on full blast, the sound of B-25 bombers flying in formation. Scout Roy setting on the far end of the log avoiding the odor of everyone, rises instantly off the log running before hitting the groud coming straight to Sterling.

Burt screams, 'Swam-swamp gn-gn-gnat." In the rush of of the action, Sterling tosses the bottle of repellant toward the middle of camp, and they all try to pounce on it at the same time. Listening and laughing, at them in mixed voices. Le me have it. n-n-no Igot it, itsmine, now. leme havesome. that thing is going to dive on us." In the thick of action Sterling turns it off, as they are doushing themselves with the potion.

Sterling calls for attention, "Hold it, hold it! Ya'll calm down. Where is the bottle of repellant? Milt jr. Thats enough, you just poured the rest of it all over yourself. Put that bottle in the trash can. *Whew!* Ya'll are powerful and protected now."

Burt asked, "rec-re-reckon w-w-we might n-nee-ne-need anotherbott-le. Just to to be be on the safe side?"

Sterling grinning raising his stethson up. "No Ya'll smell overly strong. I told ya'll this stuff was powerful. It instantly warded off that swamp gnat. That thing won't be back tonight. You scouts might ought to stoke the fire up a little before turning in for the night. A couple of scouts brings more fire wood, and places some of it on the fire, while others stack a pile by the fire. Scout Johnny said. "I can't believe how fast this stuff works. Didn't even get to see the thing."

Milt asked, "Reckon we might better put some more on just in case?"

Sterling answers, "didn't you just hear me tell Burt we would not need any more? Believe me that gnat is gone. Least of worries now."

Burt interrupting asked, "and just what do you mean by that? I'd love to be in my bed right now. Ain't no telling what Charlie has gotten Janie into. Like I said shes just like you Sterling."

Milt said, "Burt, we may not be allowed back home right now. *Whew!* This stuff stinks. I hope it wears off before Monday. Think I'll have another--darn---------I know what. Now that every thing is quiet and peaceful. Listen to the chatter of crickets, and look at the lightning bugs floating and glowing on a summer's night breeze. Lets make a pot of coffe before turning in for the night. It is only nine thirty. Listen, hear that owl, hes right over there. Across the creek is the coyotes yipping and howling. Wow! Ain't it great after all Burt?"

Burt said, Come to think of it. It is plesantly peaceful now after that swamp gnat left. Man that thing was loud. Now Milton you know how camp coffee should be. Stronger than usual. Sure could use a cup, settle my nerves."

Sterling walks to his tent grabs the other two chairs over to the camp and offers them to Milt and Burt. As they take a sip Sterling remarked, "sure is good. Just the right strength." Then they extend their tin camp cups up and out for a toast to scout camping. Some of the scouts are drinking the flavored soft drinks and making smores. They are looking into the glowing fire and talking with each other. As Burt, Milt and Sterling refill their cups with steam rising off the tops, gazing into the Western sky he notices heat lightning and clouds forming. "Aw man! I hope it ain't raining by morning. I see some heat lightning in the Western sky and clouds on the horizon. Ya'll's tents water proof?"

Scout Roy Immediately broke in and said, "My daddy treated mine with a silicone, spray that makes it plumb water proof. When we go out camping during hunting season, on weekends and some holidays, Mr. Sterling is just as fun as my daddy. I really think he is just scaring us. I'm kind of scared right now But my daddy told me about him. He told me to watch out and not to get scared. Thats why I didn't put any of this stuff on me. And now that ya'll have spread this stuff all over the camp and put a thicker coating on, I think I'll move my tent back over there by Mr. Sterling. He is just picking on us. I think that means he likes us. Yep it probably will be cloudy and light chance of rain. I really hope not. I want to play in the creek some more before leaving tomorrow morning. But I am used to seeing that lightning. Should it be raining I'm prepared to be dry, and set in my tent as long as we have to. It'll be a bit warm, thats why I have a camp fan in my pack too. Set right out side the door under the rain fly and it'll blow a rain cooled breeze wrafting right in through the fan. I am going to put my rainfly on now. One misreable feeling is the rain beating down your tent on top of you whiile you're sleeping. Have to get up in a rainstorm all soaking wet and be cold. Won't be able to build a fire either. So I'm prepared for it."

All eyes and attention is locked on scout Roy, when Sterling said. "Scout Roy I see you are the best scout out here. You are doing better than anyone here following the scout motto. Always be prepared."

Looking downward, with his hand on his forehead Burt said, "I just hope it don't rain. My tent is supposed to be water proof. Art least thats what the instructions said."

Looking at Sterling and Roy, Milt said. "But ain't all tents made to be water proof?"

Scout Roy said, while grinning. "Mr. Milton, when the factory makes them, they only treat them with a light spray of this silicone water proofiing stuff. Thats why my dad says. And as long as you don't touch the walls or roof it might not leak. But just touch them one time, and water pours in. It is best to treat them as soon as you can after buying it. Always usre the rain fly. I knew I should've put mine on. Oh well I still can. We've spent days in a tent, during down pours and never got wet. Unless one of us had to go out for something. It is really fun to camp out in the rain, especially if it is a cool or cold day. Dad had a rain fly over ours. He also had one extended out from the front with tent poles holding it up to store fire wood, and have a fire so we could keep warm."

Burt wishpers to Milt. "I think we should get outta here before the storms set in."

Sterling said, "some of you scout better add some more wood to the fire before it goes out. Burt don't worry about the rain. Look up, look out and look behind you. See all those stars shinning through out the Milky Way? That cloud bank probably won't get here until tomorrow afternoon. Then as hot and dry as it is it'll probably dissapte."

The troops are looking up and around at the sky, and Burt said." I-I-I saw, saw it lightning, and its closer now. Roy do you have a can of that spray in your tent?"

Scout Roy replied, "no sir. I treat my tent one time before a camping trip, and that is one item I can leave out. Unless we are on an extended trip. I never thought that motto could be not so thought about, until you might actually need something. See my dad teaches me about the neccessities of being parepared, as getting educated about the items you'll use. I spend a day wet, I'll catch a cold or the flu."

Burt said, "I think I just need to get home. I know what we can do, since ole western Silver gave his keys to permicious Charlie. Lets get some of these burning logs out to the middle of the sandbar arranging them in a sos pattern. Hope a satellite will spot the code and send in coast guard helicopters in. There is plenty of room for several to land and all we need is one."

Laughing at Burt, Sterling said. "Burt, Burt, I don't think that is such a good idea. Those aliens from some plantes millions and billions of miles away coulb be flying through this galaxie and spot your sos signal. Then they will dive down on us and abduct all here. I don't think I want to a gerbal for some space aliens to experiement on."

With eyes popping out, Milt asked. "You mean there could be ufos up there right now?"

Steling grinning, "yep, whats so interesting is they can disguise their space ship to look like a star. And just set up there watching us.

Scout Milt Junior asked. "How do you know that, Mister Sterling? You mean they could be watching us right now? Have you seen them before?"

Sure have, Sterling said. "And used to see them often. Be out hunting or fishing. One morning I was hiking down another trail right near here heading down to the creek bottom, to endure a frosty morning from my tree stand in hopes a deer would wander by. As I walked down the hill I saw what seemed to be a large fire that lit up a feild on the other side of the creek. I watched it a minute and thought there must be some one done reported it. Then all of a sudden I saw something that looked to be some kind of rocket blast off, into space. While watching it, as it climbed higher into the atmosphere, then it just stopped and appeared to be a star among the millions up there. I figured those aliens had been out exploring most of the night."

Raising his stethson up and glancing upwards then pointing into the sky. "Yep I think at time whoever or what ever they are interested in me. Sometimes I think I might be one disguised as a man. I find myself in hopes of meeting them in order to discover what happened. Maybe I might ev been found guilty of some crime on my home planet and was sent to Earth as punishment, and disguised as a man."

"Looking around the campers the fire continued it's flickering and reflecting on a group of frightened audience. Making eye contact with each one, and tears beginning to well up in eyes. Sitting down on the log next to Milt, still glancing at each person. Then taking the stethson off placing it on the log, looking into the sky again. "Actually I know what happened. I was the captian of a exploring vessel, on a specific mission in this area. Maybe that is why like coming to this area. It happend like this. I think my craft may have been hit by a missile from a USFA engagment. Being captian I was the commanding pilot. We were on a fun exploring mission, zipping into the Earth's atmosphere at a blinding rate of speed. Slowing down I did a couple of moves, yes a double loop and a barrel roll. Man that was fun in this slow paced environment. Planning on landing right over there in the middle of this sandbar.

Then some idiot down here reported strange lights right here in Copiah County. I kind of laughed it off as I just knew no one would believe this person. Heck I didn't think any one on this planet would believe em. Or maybe we might have got caught on radar. Then thats when it happened. I was about to get into a landing pattern, when out of the wild blue younder I was head to head with a squadron of F-14 Tomcat fighters. Slow aircraft by my standards. I was just about to send out a friendly message, and our intentions. Well one of the F-14 aricraft pilots must ev been on the panic button and fired a missle. Humans are way to nervous to fly.

In the excitement of the moment that missile struck a engine, coming close to destroying it. Good thing I didn't order my gunner to fire a degenerating shot. Could've destroyed the whole squadron with one burst. But anyway I ordered it to be shut down and turned the craft straight up and put it to the floor as ya'll would say. Then got out of Earth's gravational pull and ten minutes later crash landed on ya'll's moon. My fifteen member crew among other things donned our jet packs with some provisions and jet packed to Earth in about fifteen minutes. Slipped into this culture and Been here ever since."

A long slience and pause before anyone could say something as the whole troop had their eyes focused on Sterling. A couple of scouts slides and wiggles down the log from Sterling expecting him to transform back into a space alien for proof.

Burt wiping sweat from his forehead with wide eyes in fright said. "Sterling, Sterling, Sterling, just forget I made that suggesstion. I rather take my chances with these wild creatures. My Gosh we are stranded out here in this wilderness. Ain't no telling when we'll get home if we do. And of all things we could be led out here by some space creature pretending to be a man."

Scout Albert said, "Mister crea-----------I-I mean mister Sterling I-I did-didn't think ufo's and space aliens didn't really exists."

Burt throwing another large log on the fire, bringing it back to raging stage. Sterling staring through the licking flames at Scout Albert said, 'Shoot, whew, Albert just why don't you believe they exists? just look out into the Milky Way. It is more vast than we can probably imagine. And yet it is only a small drop within the whole universe. Ain't no telling what could be out yonder in other galaxies.. All kinds of cultures, languages and people. Tecknowledges, more advanced than ours and then others may not be. Just because you don't see um doesn't mean they are not real.

Why, ya'll followed me down here on the creek, and heard that master lion roar. When you heard that swamp gnat coming to try and get ya'll, ya rushed me like a defensive football line blitzing the quarter back. Would ya'll like for me to signal with my flash light, and get some of em down here. Then ya'll could meet um and shake hands."

Milt immediately said, "I-I-I don't think so. Story time is over. Scouts all he is telling is stories. I think we all need to turn in for the night. It is almost ten thirty."

With big teary brown eyes, Poco raises his hand. "Mister Sterling, can I sleep with you in your tent? Please, I don't think I'll sleep to good tonight."

Sterling said, while the fire is calming down. "Poco, you know you've got to earn your badge. You are okay and safe. A requirement for your badge is to be a brave scout and sleep in your own tent. Just get in there and lay down on your bed and close your eyes. Just like magic it'll be daylight and you can play in the creek before going home. I'm right here to protect you."

Poco said, "O-o-ookay. Mister Sterling good night. Good night mister Burt and mister Milt.

In unison Burt and Milt said. "Good night." And Milt continued. "Now lets all get turned in and get some shut eye."

Scout Johnny raising his hand. "Reckon we might need some more repellant on?"

Sterling answering. "No scout Johnny, every one has enough on to repel all the wild creatures over to the other side of the creek."

With that assurance every one settles down as a calm quiteness evokes the camp. Sterling pours another cup of coffee and sits down in a chair. Thirty minutes pass by in peace, when he hears a crinkling sound from a tent. He glances toward the tent seeing scout Albert rubbing his eyes while walking toward him. He then sits down on the log looking at Sterling asking. "Mister Sterling, are you a real space alien? Will I get home safley?"

Sterling reaches over and pulls the other chair close to him and motions Albert to get up and set in the chair. "See little Albert I'm here to protect ya'll. Milt knew I was the one for just such a camp out in a place like this. I promise you'll see your mommy and daddy tomorrow. Though they may not want to see, well smell you. Remember I'm your friend. Also I'm all of your friends, even Milt and Burt. We have to be just plain tuff out here. Enjoy the time out here, and especially this time of your life. Its the most magical time of all, and I'm helping with it, okay."

Scout Albert rubbing his eyes said. "Yes, mister Sterling. I'm ready to go back to bed and get some sleep and be ready for the morning. Good night mister Sterling."

Looking into his watery eyes Sterling assured him. "You're a brave scout, um good night." Albert enters his tent turns around to zip the mesh screen door and waves at Sterling in the dim fire light, and Sterling waves back. Sterling leans back in his chair taking a sip of cool coffee staring up into the starry night sky. Trying to take another sip of cold coffee and not taking it, he throws the remaing portion into the fire and walks over to his ice chest and gets a coke. Returning to the fire he puts a couple more sticks on it to keep it going for a night light. Sitting down and taking a couple of drinks from the can. The fire comes back to life. He gets up and waltzs down to the creek's edge. While walking along the edge in the full moonlight, he notices the small ripples and waves coming to shore from a light wind blowing across the water. Whats that, stopping in his tracks and listening. That stumbling and fumbling is coming from the camp.

Turning around peering back toward the camp. slipping back to the camp site listening to the comotion, he pauses. As he studies the scene making out Burt's form through a dying flame, he picks up a stick and begins to stir the ashes, reviving the fire momentarily. In nothing but his house slippers and breifs, he stumbles to Milt's tent.

"*PST! pst, pst Milton.*"

Milt answers "Yea that you Burt?"

Burt responds, "Yes its me. Get out here. That idiot, our leader has vanished."

Milt runs out of his tent, with house slippers and striped boxers on. He immediately grabs a couple of sticks of wood and throws them on the fire. Both stands by the fire trying to see out in the darkness around camp.

Burt asked, "where could he be? His tent is still up, but he is not in it."

Milt answered, "How the heck do I know where Jesse James went. I ain't about to venture out there to find him. No telling whats out there waiting for our hides."

Sterling approaches closer in the shadows of darkness around camp. Milt and Burt sits down on the log, folding their arms, looking up into the sky. In the stillness of the moment Sterling pushes the on button of the remote. With the sounds of war drums and galloping horses, Sterling runs into camp yelling. "*Milt! Burt! Get those younguns out and have them lay flat behing these logs with their hands folded behind their heads. We're under an Indian attack, hurry!*" Sterling rushes to his tent grabs his Ruger .22 magnum revolver, and a couple of Bowie style Damascus steel knives. He turns the volume up to make the attack seem closer, as he runs back into camp. The scouts screaming crying, getting down by the logs. Sterling hands Milt and Burt the kinves and orders. "Get to the back of camp, and don't let any of those braves in. We'll get scalped.!" As the sound of horses hoofs beating with each quick gallop and Indians yipping and hollering, Sterling dives into the sand by a tent and fires six rounds into a tall dirt cliff across the creek. As the attack intensifies with gun shots sounding off on the tape, Sterling runs back to his tent and retrieves two arrows and rushes back to the action sticking the arrows into the log by Scouts George and Bob. Laying back down in the sand he fires three more rounds off into the dirt bank. Then gradually fades the the attack. Sterling rises up, placing his hands on the top of his thighs standing up and walks through the small camp. "Okay! Okay! Ya'll can stop all the crying and hollering. Everyone get up and sit on the logs. Any one hurt?" Sobing and crying they get up and sits down on the logs. "Don't see any blood from anyone. Just sit here while I go and check on Milt and Burt." Walking the few stepts to the rear of camp he saw two frozen forms bow legged with arms extended upwards weilding the knives as if in a defensive position. Sterling hobbles in the shifting sand pushing his stethson up a little while eyeing Milt and Burt up and down. He reaches up slowly taking the knives from their hands. Pulling their arms down, "Milt, Burt snap out of it and lets get back in camp. Can't leave those scouts alone." They slowly turn to look at Sterling. Speechless they follow stiff legged back to the camp fire and sits down. Sterling along with a couple of scouts dip paper towels in a bucket of creek water and wipes their fore heads. The cool water brings them back to their senses.

Burt asking. "Sterling, Sterling! Is the attack over? I didn't see the first warrior. The scouts okay? I-I-I jus-just hop-hop- hope, this esc-esc-escap-e--de is over. I-I-I thou-thoug-thoug-ht we-we were gon-gonners."

Milt lookng the scouts over, "You-you kids all right?" They all nodding up and down.

CHAPTER 5

PEACE TREATY

Sterling standing in front of them with his revolver in the holster on his hip and hands placed on each hip, with right leg slightly bent, and leaning foward, looking at Milt and Burt. "The scouts are safe. Lucky no one got nabbed by a brave. Well ya'll certainly put of a defense didn't ya." Ya'll listen up. Now I've got to go and smoke the peace pipe with them, or they'll be back and this time we'll be lucky to survive."

"Milt asks, "how do you know they will allow you in their camp? Especially after you've shot at them?"

Pointing at the two replica cedar arrows stuck in the log. "Thats how I know."

Upon seeing the arrows, Burt exclaims, *"Ow my gosh! Sterling, its a wonder any of us are alive!"*

Scouts George and Bob instantly begins crying and George said. "They were shooting at me. Just a little higher, and that arrow would a went through my head. I want my mommy, I want my mommy. I wanna go home."

Sterling gives both of them a comforting pat and rub on their heads assuring them. "Those two arrows were not intended to hit any one. Ya'll just calm down and we'll be alright." Then looking at Milt and Burt as thier faces just flushes white with panic and faint. "Look you two, I need ya'll to regroup yourselves, cause I've got just a short time to make it to the big smoke party. Now ya'll listen carefully to my instructions. There are two braves out there watching ya'll to make sure you don't try anything funny. Of all things do not touch their arrows. If anyone touches them then all of ya are scalped. It'll be a massacre right here in Copiah county."

"But," Milt whined, "About how long will you be gone? Reckon you'll be back before daylight?"

Sterling answered. "Oh sure, won't be gone much more-n- a hour. This particular tribe makes up their mind's up quick."

Burt said, "Please! Please! Please! Smoke a lot with them. Do you really have to go out there leaving us alone?"

Sterling staring out into the darkness, taking in the out line of tall trees in the distance, glowing in the full moon. Then looks at Burt, while putting his hands on his hips and leans foward slightly on a bent knee. Pulling his stethson down, answers. "No I don't. I can send you if you'd like the experience. You know good-in- well this has to be done. Heck, haven't ya'll watched Wagon Train, Gun Smoke? Ole Matt Dillon is always making some kind of peace treaty and deals with all kinds of people. Also the Cartwrights. It has to be done. Shoot! I can send any one of ya'll to do it. They are set up right on the road by that mound."

Burt said. "Yes I still watch those shows, but that is just television entertainment. No! No! NO! If this has to be done just go out there and do it. Please get back as soon as you can. Any-an- any wa-way, I-I don't see why-why they would wan-wan-want m-me. I don't have much hai-hai-hai-r, other than around the side of my head. I-I-I'll probably wil-will lose i-i-it before any Indians cap-capt-u-re us."

Sterling straightens up with arms and hands outward said. "Well Burt, you're the perfect size to be tied on the burn pole." Burt falls backwards. "Ya'll pour a bucket of creek water on him. I've got to get on over there and smoke the pipe. I'll be back after while. Remember ya'll are being watched during this. So don't touch those two arrows." Sterling turns and walks out of camp with his flash light pointing the way. *Aw, man, I don't need this light on. The moon has the whole land scape lit up in it's yellowish glow.* A fresh breeze flavored with the savory sent of the creek, makes him stop for a minute. Walking down to a point of the sandbar, where it meets the creek, *can't be out here too long. They'll be in hysterics and panic.* Approaching the little point a owl hoots and takes wing. He notices a wing feather floating in the yellow glow and lights gently on the creeks edge by the sand bar. He hurries to it reaching down and picks it up. All of a sudden feeling something flowing down his left hand, he wipes it on his forehead and along his left cheek. *What! That don't feel like water.* Turning the flash light on the beam illumnates the spot in his palm is oozing blood. Must have scratched and slightly cut mysefl when I dived into the sand. Maybe scraping it on George's tent peg. Oh well ain't too bad just now beginning to bleed a little. Need to be getting back to camp. Don't want to leave them alone too long. Dropping the feather, and strolls a few feet toward camp he turns back to pick up the feather. Need something to tell the troops and their fearless leaders what happened at the smoking event. Hey got blood, now I got it, get on back to camp. Approaching the camp, he hears Burt. Stopping short of camp he listens to the conversation. Burt said. "Also Milt you and I are scared, and these boys will be so impacted by this, they'll never be right again. Plus add the fact that he is some alien from some undiscovered planet out there somewhere in the universe. No telling how far out. He is stuck down here with us and we've known him quite a few years. Like you said a minute ago I too wished we'd went to the scout reservation. We wouldn't be dealing with a bunch of Indian spirits wanting our hair. We are just sruck out here in this wilderness and no way to get home. Plus it could take days for us to walk home."

Scout Bob sobbing again, whimpers, "Yea mister Milt, one of those Indians was shooting at me. See where that arrow hit the log? Right by where I was laying. Wha-wha-wha I just want my mommy."

Scout Robert said, It was kind of fun being in an real Indian attack. Especially when none of them could get by Sterling. I bet he knocked several off their horses. Man can he shoot. Ain't nothing got a chance in front of him. I just hope I can be that good a shot one day."

Milt and Burt along with the rest of the troops stares in disbelief at Robert, then Milt said. "Well for your information, young scout, being attacked and threatned to be scalped and massacred isn't the fun of fun for cub scouts. That giant escaped lion, the flying swamp creature. Aw what ever it is. For all we know they could've got off of his ufo when it got blasted. Even his driving a vehicle shows that is possible. And now those renegade Indian spirits wants our heads. And of all things Sterling gave his keys to Charlie, when she demanded them. Shows who wears the pants around their home. And there is no way I'm hiking thorugh that dangerous wilderness. Ann hopefully will get a search and rescue party out after us by tomorrow afternoon if Charlie hasn't led her off anywhere. I'm staying right here by the fire and in the middle of the repellant. Put some more wood on the fire, get it stoked up. It's kind of cool now."

Burt said, 'I don't think this is much fun either, but you, Bob with his exterme prepardness and Sterling think it is kind a funny. I can tell you one thing, you won't catch me out here again with Wyat Earp. In fact we should be at home in our own beds, sleeping right now. It's almost two o' clock and we're up and hugging this fire for protection. Plus there is a couple of warriors out there just waiting for us to make a move. Ain't no telling when Little Joe will be back. Also in fact Milt we should be coaching little league base ball and umpiring the bigger leagues. But naw! We have to be on a deserted desert like sandbar with a small creek flowing through it. My nerves are not going to hold up much lnger. Heck the ambein I took a few hours ago hasn't had any effect. Whats taking him so long. He done had enough time to smoke several pipe fulls of tobacco."

Sterling then strides pridefully into the camp. "Every one okay? A couple of the scouts jumps as if they had been struck by a lightning bolt. Milt and Burt turns to see what caused their startle with eyes wide open.

Milt said, "Whew! glad you're back Did you make a peace treaty with them?"

Sterling walks over to his chair setting down pushing his stethson up. "Listen carefully you're going to have do what I tell you. Or you're gonners. Now-----"

Scout Albert interrupts, "Gee! mister Sterling you are bleeding. You must've been hit by an arrow. Just look at the blood."

Milt exclaimed, "What! Gosh! Its your hand."

Scout Roy said. "Mister Sterling you're not going to die and leave us out here with those Indian spirits are you?. Please stop the bleeding."

Scout Bob jumps up running to Sterling crying. Sterling wants to pick the little chubby fellow up but the scents stops it. Sterling reaches down pushing the scout's cap up in a comforting motion. "What is it scout Bob?"

Scout Bob sobbing rubbing his eyes, "Mister Sterling, Those Indians were wanting me. Two arrows hit the log right by where I was laying. I want my mommy."

Sterling reassures them. "Ya'll can calm down now. There is nothing to be scared of now. Just do as I tell you."

Burt interupting. "Sterling what happened to you out there. Look at your face."

Sterling pulling his stethson down said, 'Ya'll sit back down. I've got to have your undivided attention. Poco! Do'nt grab those arrows. They have to stay in the log. It's part of their signature now for the treaty settled on."

"Burt shouted. "Look! Ya'll leave those arrows alone. I don't want to see anyone even look at them again."

Scout Edward asked. "How did you cut your hand?"

Sterling said,. "Okay every one wants to know about my hand, its really nothing. After smoking the final round of the peace pipe, for the accepted agreement, we had to seal it in blood. You know take your own knife and cut into the palm of your hand. Then each warrior cuts his hand, and you shake hands with each member of the council. If the blood clots you have to cut it again even deeper. As we drug the knives across our hands blood began flowing and squirting, turnning the ground red in some spots. I must've went across a vein and it squirted into my face. So we all had a good laugh to ease the sting and pain.'

Milt wide eyed said. "Sterling that is a nasty cut. It may need a few stitches."

Sterling lifts his hand to the glowing camp fire acting as if he is opening and inspecting it, wrenching in a perceived pain. "Aw, don't really look that bad, just a lot of dried clotted blood. Remember there was a large number of warriors. I'll look at it closer in my tent under better lighting. If it needs a stitch or two I'll do it. Like I said we all have our first aid kits. Actually shouldn't need more-n-half a dozen. I might as well go and get it. Set here by the fire and go to work on it.

The whole troop looks at Sterling in disbelief, as he gets up. Burt said, "But Sterling, I think you should wit until Charlie comes back to get us. She can rush you to the emergency room."

Pushing his stethson up, "Burt you know I've got to do this. Should this cut get infected and I pass out in a fever, can ya'll get out in one peice? We've got to get past those Indian spirits."

Burt answered. "I think I know where the trail to get out is. Just follow that log road right up there. It'll lead to the camps' gravel road right to the camp house. To get past those ghosts we'll just break out in a dead run and hope we can out run them."

"O ha-ha-ha. Burt. Really none of ya'll would survive that. Ya'll haven't given me the chance to go over the laws concrning the treaty. Let me explain it before I sew my hand."

"Yea one other thing Sterling. In the attack while ago, and you were shooting at them, that was the most deafning noise I've ever heard. I'm going to have to make an appointment with my ear doctor should we get out. Plus while this is on my mind I'm going to need some psychiatric help. But any way while you were shooting at them, did you wound or even kill any of those savages?"

Sterling glaring in a supposed anger, while they all looked on. In a Eastwood smile just before gunning down some outlaws. "First those are no savages. How would you like it, to be called a steretyped name like paleface?" Then turning his gaze to Milt and the scouts. "Do Ya'll!" They are sure Sterling is angry because of the question. A bunch of big eyed boys are shaking their wrinkled heads from side to side. "Well, then neither do they. Gosh my hand is stinging and throbbing. Might'ev cut a ligament or a nerve. Winching, "so those braves and the cheif knows me. They know I'm not going to disturb them, even when I fire my gun around their mound, while hunting. Ya'll know their bodies are buried there. While I was firing to to scare that lion into escaping across the creek, evey one of ya'll had to start screaming and hollering. A couple of ya'll had to break into a charge to the creek. Those spirits thought they were under attack and got stirred up. After they retaliated their attack, then I was invited to join in for the peace pipe smoking and working out a peace treaty. Ya'll want the deails, you'd better listen carefully."

Milt rises from the chair and begins a worried panicked pacing back and forth. "Milt you need to sit back down and listen to me. Okay when I arrived at the mound, they bound my hands behind my back with leather strips, for safety. Then I was blind folded and led into their camp. I was set down by a couple of braves folding my legs cross ways. Then the blind fold was removed. I sat there in the darkness, only the shadow of the mound reflected in the setting moon. A minute or two later a rattling sound came from my immediate right front. As it got louder, I heard drum beats. The rattling sound went around and around a certian area and then back to me. The drum beats got louder, then a chanting lasting quite a few minutes. As it was ending the whole tribal war council appeared seated around a large raging fire. I was setting by two sun dried brown skinned braves, about half a foot taller than me And a mite more muscular. Kinda smelt like they hadn't had a bath in ages. A minute later the cheif emerges from his teepee, and straightens up. Tall, dark and confident, in his war dress. Which was of long deer skin pants with fringe waving down ward. His sheild of deer bones over his fringed deer skin shirt, is just amazing, with the head dress of feathers from several local species of predatory birds, just cascaded down rearward. He glanced at me with a slight smile and blink of his dark eyes. Motioning with his right hand toward me and nodded, then set down. A couple of braves cut the leather straps from my hands. Then the cheif raised his left hand palm toward me and said. How, Ole Silver. I raised mine and said, How, Cheif, Red Tail Hawk. I come in peace. He nodded toward me in acceptance and reterived the pipe a long stemmed afair with a corn cobb bowl the size of a ceral bowl set atop it at mid length. He began stuffing it with rabbit tobacco, when a brave tried to stop him. He whispered something to the cheif. Then Cheif Red Tail Hawk motioned me to his teepee."

The boys are aghast as fright widened their eyes. Milt and Burt stood up and walked to the fire to warm themselves as the night air was cooling down a few degrees.

"I entered his teepee, he bowed to me and motioned for me to set down on his bear skin rug, as he set up right with legs crossed. He informed me that the braves wanted to capture the tender foots and put them in cages just big enough to stand in. They wanted to have a little fun with you two. Tie ya'll up on a pole and have the medicine man to cast a spell on ya. Turn ye into swamp rats. One even suggested to turn ya into large bull frogs and roast ye legs. Cause some of them are hungry."

Milt rushes into his tent and grabs a cloth wash rag. He returns and dips it into the bucket of creek water, then squeezes it out, and wipes his forehead. Burt sits down on a log, propping his elbows on his knees and putting his forehead in his palms shaking back and forth. He slides his hand over his face, looking back up at Sterling. "I can't stand this anymore. If I just had my car phone I'd call Janie and have her to call the coast guard to rescue us." Then they all start crying.

Sterling commanded, "okay, okay, ya'll hush and listen." Milt pacing back and forth mopping his forehead with the damp rag. "Look ya'll don't have to worry about that. I explained to Cheif Red Tail Hawk what happened. I told him. "Cheif, it's my fault I forgot to tell them about you and this mound. Do with me what you will. It's not their fault. But earlier when I brought the supplies to the creek and made a visit to this mound, I figured the braves would recogonize me, and things would go alright."

Cheif Red Tail Hawk told me. "Silver, you I, and my tribe be friends, we be up tight. But tenderfoots alarmed my warriors, had them thinking of being attacked. Now things be okay, we go back out, smoke peace pipe. Make peace again." He motioned me to get up. When I got up, he went out first, then me. He addressed the war council by raising his hands pointing at me then out into the wilderness. "Me, Cheif Red Tail Hawk regret great mistake with Ole Silver. Swamp wild cat caused alarm. So we get on smoking peace pipe." He took the pipe putting it between his lips and the medicine man lit it as he drew the smoke into his lungs, then let it out in a great white cloud. He then passed it to his right. That brave took it and drew a deep draw. When it came to me I took a really deep draw and almost choked as I let the smoke out. The brave from whom it came patted me on my back and laughed. The brave I passed it to on my left, was Brave Strong Floating Feather. He was reluntant, because he wanted to regroup for a second attack. However at the cheif's urging he finally took in a shallow draw. After a couple of more rounds, and a lot of rabbit tobacco burned, and smoked up, cheif Red Tail Hawk handed the pipe back to the medicine man. Then he motioned me to stand by the blazing fire and face him. He said, "Go, back to your camp. Have great pow wow about regretted message. But for peace, a great sacrifice is to be had." He handed to me, two long leather strips. "Take these, bound scout Edward, hand and foot. Have other troops carry him here. Medicine man then bring him here and set him down. The other troops sit around great fire. Medicine man put more logs on. Have great roaring fire, light whole site up. Braves tie tall slender belly up on burn pole. Medicine man put five piles of wood around it."

Burt jumps up about to make a run. Sterling shouted. "Hold on Burt! You'll be a gonner for sure. Just sit back down and listen." Milt dips his rag in the bucket of water, rings it out. "Well cheif Red Tail Hawk continued. "Brave Strong Floating Feather will wrastle Short round belly over great fire. If brave Strong Floating Feather throws short round belly, medicine man light fire under slender belly. Me Cheif Red Tail Hawk cut some hair off Scout Edward. If round Belly throws brave Strong Floating Feather, medicine man put fire out, and I put band around Scout Edward's head with one feather in it." Milt pacing back and forth faster, wiping and mopping his whole head and face with his rag. He rushes to the ice chest grabbing a hand full of ice and wraps his rag around it.

Then stops and stares at Sterling. "Why, why, why me. Just why should we have to go through this?"

Poose sha, Burt takes a sip on his coke. "I've got to have something to drink. It really needs to be stronger than this. Sterling this can't be what you agreed on."

Sterling said, "Well it is as Cheif Red Tail Hawk determined, He makes the rules. If Brave Strong Floating Feather throws Milt you'll feel some heat and Scout Edward will loose a swath of hair. So if Milt throws Brave Strong Floating Feather then the fire will be put out and Scout Edward gets a feather from the Cheif's war head dress. It makes up for the lost hair. So I'm figuring it'll be a five round match."

Burt whines, "Now, now, now yo-you-you know good in wel-well, tha-tha-tha-that Milt Is is gonna ge-get-get wupped. Scout Edward will be bald headed with no more hair to be cut. Wha- wha- what then? And I-I-I'll be-be-be Roa-roas-roasted. I-I-I just can-can't tak-take any more of-of this. I just want to be back at ho-ho-home wit-wit-with my Jan-Janie and be in our bed. And Day light ain't coming for a while yet."

Scout Edward tries to get closer to Sterling. Wiping tears and choking a little. "Mister Sterling, please don't let that Indian chief pick me. I don't want to be tied up and have to sit by him while he cuts all my hair off. Waa, waa, waa, I want my mommy, I want my mommy, waa-waa."

Then Milt said. "Sterling, look, you've got to go back out there see that cheif and smoke some more of that pipe and make other arrangements. Tell'em we'll be really quiet going out. Really walking slow. We'll even tippy toe out."

"Ha, ha, ha, ha, Ya'll calm down now." while pushing his stethson up.

Burt asked, "What do you mean calm down? We are about to enter their excution exercise. How do I know? Because Milt don't know a thing about wrestling. Little Edward will get his veins cut out of his head. I'll be cooked. Look! We are responsible for getting those younguns home safely. So whats so funny?"

Sterling sets down pulling his stethson off leans back. "Ha-ha-hahahahahah." Putting the hat back on pulling the front down looking at them sobbing and whinning. "Ya'll haven't heard the rest of the story yet. Just listen. I didn't agree to that and asked cheif Red Tail Hawk to start another round of peace pipe smoking, and hear me out."

"Um!" He groaned. "Okagunawaaahoaka wookaweeee." Drums began a fast paced beat. Then the medicine man began his chant waving his rattle and dancing around the pow wow, right in front of us. Then sauntered and two stepped to the beats on his way to the cheif handing him the pipe. Cheif Red Tail Hawk filled it with tobacco and took a draw as the medicine man lit it. Me, Cheif Red Tail Hawk will hear Ole Silver. After he take smoke. So when it came to me, I took as deep a draw as I could and handed it over to brave Strong Floating Feather. But again he did not want to do it. He still wanted to lead out for an attack and get ya'll or continue the wrasteling match. Cheif Red Tail Hawk crossed his arms and leaned foward then touched the ground. patting it. Then raised up lifting his hands to the sky and waving back and forth. Then Brave Strong Floating Feather laid his bow and arrow quiver filled with arrows down between us. *Whew!* I thought. When the pipe came back to cheif Red Tail Hawk, he handed it to medicine man. This medicine man took one last deep draw. Letting the smoke slowly out it drifted upwards in a circle and vanished. Cheif Red Tail Hawk pointed at me, waving his hand directing me to stand in front of the fire. "We, now shall hear Ole Silver. Speak Ole Silver."

Milt still pacing back and forth with the frozen rag to his forehead. The troops and Burt with wide eyed hysteria, jaws agasht and mouths open eyes glued on Sterling. Sterling rises up from his chair and stands by the fire. "Standing there in front of cheif Red Tail Hawk, I addressed the whole war council. Cheif Red Tail Hawk, and braves, fearless, invisible and swift as the wind. Warriors, the best of the best. It is with my complete earntness, to plead for mercy, and light punishment on my company. They, even their leaders are scared, because they have no experience in the wilderness. They are actually on a leisure, fun over night trip. The great adventure began up on the road at pale face's hunt camp. Oh I forgot, I did Just as I was supposed to do. I warned them to be really quiet, when they approached this sacred area. I did not intend for them to make a mistake and cause alarm. But you know that great swamp cat, started this whole mistaken act of war. Those camped on fast flowing stream are just tender foots, with a couple older, gray stray cats leading them. None of them could out perform any of you. Yes I understand you want a sacrifice for them to pass back through when sun is high in the sky. And they need to return to their home land as ya'll would also want to pass to your home land. But most if not all of you have never left this area now or in the past when you romed here in both body and spirit. They have not harmed the environment nor littered it. You have my oth in the cut of palms with hand shake they shall leave it as clean as it was. If you cheif Red Tail Hawk, and great members of war council setting here would just receive some hair from each of them. I seek on their behalf you receive a portion of their hair. And allow them to pass by on their way out to pale face's hunting camp and dissappear as you shall also."

"Ummmmmm," Cheif Red Tail Hawk began, "humpawoopygupa womba hum okawanga ricco." Then the medicine man came out dancing a jig around each of us as the drums began beating to a happier tune. The cheif tall and confident got up and walked to me reaching out for a hand shake. The whole war council began dancing for peace because it was made. Then Cheif Red Tail Hawk raised his hands and the braves came back to attention. Cheif motioned for every one to sit down.

When Brave Strong Floating Feather sat down next to me he patted me on my back. He said to me. "Great Speech from pale face tougue. Hope it ain't forked. Didn't really want to wrastle. Last pale face I wrastled threw me in great fire. Hair burned off, do not grow again. This easy way to get some." Then here comes medicine man jumping on one leg then another shaking his rattle over us. He touched me with the rattle. Brave Strong Floating Feather said. "That means he like you. Don't have to chant many nights without sleep over wounded tender foots. All be quiet now. No hollering out in pain." Then medicine man danced around the fire a couple of times and vanished, and as the rattling gradually vanished with him Cheif Red Tail Hawk rose from his place. He said. Ole Silver make great peace treaty. Ole Silver may go back to camp in peace. When sun half way in sky, ritual starts on trail leading to pale face's crowded land. Thank Great Spirit for peace."

Milt stops the pacing holding his frozen rag to his fore head. "*Whew!* Won't have to be in the ring after all. What do we have to do now?

Sterling pulls his hat down and stares out into the darkness contemplating. "Well here is the final agreement. *Gosh my hand is hurting and stinging.* I've got to get it sewed up. But first I'll tell ya'll what we'll have to do. Remember it is to be followed to the tee. It was finalized and signed with our cut and blood trading, with handshakes. Any one who violates the treaty, I'll cut the survivors of what will happen. If any, so ya'll listen carefully. We'll have to be as quite as possible packing up. Be sure the fire is completely out and all trash picked up. On our way out we'll have to move slowly and quietly. When we reach a certian point medicine man will stop me. I'll be in the lead, Milt you'll be right behind me and the scouts line up behind Milt. Burt you'll have to bring up the rear."

Burt whinned, "But Sterling, Sterling, Sterling why can't I be right up there behind you? It is always me."

"Well," Sterling said with a grin. "I can put you up front on point, so you can be first to take an arrow should any one mess up."

Burt said, "never mind Sterling, I'll stay in the rear. Might be safer in that place any way."

Milt said, 'Yea Burt since you are the tallest you'll be able to see over us. If you spot something amiss you can quickly let us know. I actually don't think Sterling pays much attention to where he is going anyway. Just think, Ann could possibly still be out somewhere following Charlie. I just hope Abby our nineteen year old neice, who is baby sitting for her is alright. Maybe lttle Joni is sleeping peacefully right now."

Sterling interrupting, "allright ya'll hush and listen. This has to be done right or all of ye be gonners. So when we arrive at the mound where medicine man and which ever brave he chooses will stop our train. They will communicate to me exalty when to halt. Then the brave will walk across the trail. Now ya'll won't be able to see them but they'll make themselves visible to me. So we can get on with the ritual." He then holds the owl feather up. "See this feather? Cheif Red Tail Hawk plucked it from his head dress handing it to me for use in the ceremony of safe passage." Pulling his stethson down, "Okay, when we meet them I'll take a couple of steps forward and observe and direct the cuttting as desired. When I step foward and turn around I will draw this knife out. Since you are right behind me you'll be the feather bearer, all the way to the sacred spot. When I turn and face you, you'll hand me the feather and I'll hand you the knife.

Then I'll direct Burt to come foward in front of you. I'll hand Burt the feather and the cut will began. Milt you'll began the cut right off the top of his head. Oops, I forgot you don't have any hair on top. Might have to fillet a strip of scalp or hide."

Burt interrups, "Sterling you just can't allow that to happen. My gosh It's getting harder all the time to get outta here, and back to real civilization."

Sterling calls his attention back. "Aw, Burt they'll probably be happy with what ever they can get from around your head. But anyway, When Burt's hair is cut down to the skin, Milt will turn and hand the knife back to me. And Burt will pass the feather back to Milt. Then Burt will exchange the feather for the knife. Burt you will cut the top first, down to about a three quarters of an inch. All the way back to the bottom of his neck. You should taper it as you cut and trim. Then cut only the right side of his head, all the way down to where it comes out his skin. Leaving his left side as is with only about a sixtenth or eight of a inch gap separating the unity sign of the strip. When done you will hand me the knife and Milt will hand me the feather. Then the next scout behind you, Milt will stept foward. I'll hand the knife to Milt and he will cut the scout's hair in the same pattern. Exept every other one will be cut on both sides. Right side to the skin and left side about half way. The singifiance of the short stip down the center to the base of the neck ties this group into one unified pack. When the last one is done and no one has screamed and hollered, or even tried to run then we can pass on through quietly and softly. The way of peace."

Milt still wiping his head and face with the half frozen wet rag. *Whew!* What a relief, that this is the agreement. Should be quiet easy to do. I'd rather lose my hair than this whole company. Because that wratleing match was all dependant on me."

Sterling said. "Well Milt you are the fearless leader who wanted such an experience."

Burt said, "if they want my hair then I'll be glad to give it to them. Just don't cut my scalp and hide. What is it about Indians, All they want is scalp and hair. Ain't it funny that there are all kinds of wild animals running free out here and they have plenty of hair. I guess we're just easier targets."

Sterling said, "yep this is the final agreement. One little mistake, whimper or holler, ye all are gonners and scalped entirely. Now the matter is done, I've got to sew up my hand." He then walks to his tent retreving his compact first aid kit. He takes some of Charlene's left over makeup and makes the scratch appear worse than it really is. He returns to camp, sits down on the edge of his chair pushing his hat up leaning forward, laying the hook on a stick by the fire.

Burt, watching Sterling intently. "Sterling, it's only a few hours till daylight. If you can wait Charlie will take you to the er. I'll get your pickup key and drive it home for you. Milt and the scouts can pack out in the back and ride."

Milt said encouraging. "Yes Sterling, I think you should just wrap your hand in a ice pack and wait until we can get you to the er."

Pushing his hat up and staring at each of them he said. "Look! Don't tell me ya'll don't watch Gun Smoke, Bonanza, or the Virginian, and other westerns. Ole Josey Whales, The Duke, Matt Dillon, along with the Cartwrights don't go to the doctor when they get nicked by a bullet. Or cut by some Indian. Why heck no, they pull a bullet with thier teeth from it's case and pours the gun powder in the wound and strikes up a match and cortorizes it. Yep that gun powder lights right up, while biting down on the bullet. They even sew a cut up themselves. Got to be tough and prepared out here. Now if ya'll want to, you can watch. Might learn something." Leaning back in his chair, stretching out his right leg. Sliding his hand into the pocket of his jeans, brings out a couple of .22 rifle cartridges with loosen bullets, holding them up. He takes one between his teeth and pulls it out. He pretends to pour the gun powder into his cut, but letting it spill to the ground behind his hand. Then he tosses the case into the fire, and takes the bullet out of his mouth, He said, "You boys need to stoke up the fire a little. Put a couple more logs on it. When I get my hand sewed up I may roast a couple of hotdogs, to take my mind off the pain. Also Powing wowing and smoking peace pipe with a bunch of dead Indians works up a man's appitiate. That hook ought to be hot enough by now."

Milt asked, "why did you put the hook by the fire?"

Sterling answering, "well Milt ole pal, I'm going to tell you. My hand is about to kill me now especially when I lit the gun powder in it. The fire sterilizes the hook. I don't think you'd want me to get infectedd and pas out for about four days. Would ya?"

Milt said, "no, we've got to get outta here today. If them Indians will allow us."

Sterling said, "well let me do what I have to do, so I can help us get back to civilization in one peice."

With a worried, concerned appearance, Milt said. "Let me have a closer look at your hand." Sterling holds his hand up and Burt saunters closer for a look. Inspecting the wound he exclaimed. *"My gosh Sterling!* How could you cut your hand that bad, and gapped open."

Burt sauntering closer for a look, also exclaims. *"Sterling!* You think you are going to sew that bad a wound up? Your hand ought to be so sore now, you couldn't even touch it. Again allow me to wrap it in ice and like I said we'll have Charlie rush you to the hospital first thing. We'll give them Indians all our hair, just to get you out safely. You could possibly lose that hand."

Scout Roy interrurpted with out raising his hand. "Mister Sterling, please wait and let us get you to a doctor, please."

Sterling looks down at Scout Roy telling him. "It'll be all right Roy. This camp out has turned into a extereme camp out. Even a scout going for the eagle badge would have a hard time getting through this. See ya'll aren't prepared as you thought. I think ya'll should rethink your motto. Well that fish hook is probably really hot now. Letme get it." He raises back up on the edge of his chair leans over and picks the fish hook up. Juggling it in his hand and blowing on it. "Ooh, ooh, ha, ha," Then drops it in the sand. Picking it up blowing the sand off. "Yep it's hot enough hope I blew all the sand off. Could cause a bad infection." He pretends to string it up and leans closer to the fire light to see.

Scout Johnny said, "Mister Sterling thats going to burn and hurt worse ain't it?"

Then Scout Bob said, "Mister Sterling sir, please just wait until you can get to the hospital. This is bad."

Sterling said, "Nope, its got to be done now. I'm already in pain, so whats a little more? The hot hook will cortorize the wound in case the gun powder didn't get all of it. The hook will also cortorize the outer area as I pull it through. If ya'll want to watch then spread out a little more and give me some breathing and grunting room." Then, he takes the bullet back between his teeth. He pretends to bite down on the bullet and pull the hook and line through the wound. He glances upwards, squinting. "Oooo ahhhhhh, umumumumum. Whe! That one is through. Take a breather and go for another. Milt can you or Burt bring me a paper towel or two and that bucket of water? If we have enough ice put a few peices in it. Two or three more stitches and I'll be through." Milt grabs the towels and Burt throws some ice in the bucket of creek water and rushes to Sterling sloshing some of it out. "Ummm, ummmm, ooooooccch oooch, ou, ou, ou aw, aw, aw" gasping for breath. As the hook seems to come through his flesh, he rolls back his head letting the hat fall off. "Breathing hard, "thank you Burt and Milt." unrolls a couple of sheets ripping them off. Dunking it in the water squeezing it out he wipes his forehead. The whole group looking upon him as he bites down harder it seems on the bullet and grunts. "One more pull and that should do it." Ooooooh, ahahahah, umumumumum. closing his eyes really tight as he seems to jerk the hook through and out. Then lifts up looking at it. He upsnaps the knife sheath pulling out the knife and cuts the line and spits the bullet into the fire. Then replaces and snaps the sheath closed. "Ah, now it is done." he picks up his hat putting it on as he stands. "I need a cold drink now." Burt rushes to the ice chest and returns with a coke handing it to Sterling. "Thank you."

Burt said. "Any thing else I can do? I have a pack of bc's in my tent. Extra strength if you'd like one. I just don't think you should've done that."

Sterling said. "Well I could use one, the pain is great now." He pulls off a few more sheets of towels and dunks he in the water squeezes it out and wrps it around his hand, while inspecting it. "It'll be all right, when the pain subsides." Burt hands him the pack of bc. swallowing it down. "Okay ya'll its three thirty. If ya'll are going to ern your camping badge you'd better get in your tents and get some sleep."

Scout Albert asked. "But mister Sterling what if those Indians decide to attack again?"

Sterling assured him, and the whole outfit. "They won't attack again. The agreement has been shaken in blood. I have their word and they have mine. And ya'll better do as I instruct. But remember there are two braves out there watching, to be sure those arrows are not removed. Now its time to bed down again." With a relief they go into their tents.

CHAPTER 6

Ritual Coming

Burt mumbles as he enters his tent. 'I wish I was at home safe and sound, sleeping in my own bed next to Janie. I sure hope she is home right n-nnow. I sure wouldn't be smelling like some dead animal and a live one done peed on me. Plus I wouldn't have to fool with those Indian ghosts. No body better not tell me ghosts don't exists. For all I know he may be done beamed down some ET, and it is roaming this sandbar. No telling what they might do to us, before those Indians get us. Of all things we may be out here with one, our fearless leader. Something is wrong with him anyway. I always knew he was strange. I just want to go home. Its too dark and hot in here. Guess I'll have to take another ambiem now. And still have a hard time going to sleep. Plus can't sleep to long, or as he says it, we'll be gonners for sure. Whew, I'm sweating, and the repellant seems to be getting stronger too.'

A half hour passes by and all is quiet. Ashew, ashew, ashew, hac, hac, aswhew, aswhew, coming from Burt's tent. Sterling sloshes around in the melting ice for a pack of hotdogs. Getting one out, then running the stick through it he sits down and lowers it into the small normal camp fire. He is gazing into the fire as the weiner roast, as the wood crackles as it burns. A zip, zip, brings his thoughts back as Milt walks to him and sets down on a log. Sterling sips a swallow of coke, Milt asks. "Mind if I sit up with you a few minutes?" I'm just not sleepy yet."

"I guess, probably no one is too sleepy yet. Been a long exciting night. But they'll eventually go to sleep. In about another half hour I'll turn in for the morning. Get some sleep and rest for the ritual."

Checking his watch in the flickering light. "Well it is four o clock. You know it's been a long time since I've been up most all night. If I was at home I'be sleeping. In about an hour the old alarm would be sounding off. Plus the fact ole Strong, um um whoever----------"

"Strong Floating Feather."

"Oh yea, Floating Feather wanted to wrastle me. *Whew!* I'm glad you got that changed. I am grateful you persaded them to go light on us. In fact we may be better off on the Scout reservation. Certainly would be safer." Oh well I really need to turn in for a while. Don't want to over sleep. Got about three and a half hours to sleep and then have to get up. Can't stand the thought of over sleeping and those Indians coming quietly into camp and dragging all of us off."

"Aw Milt, ain't no need to go to bed yet. You said yourself that you weren't sleepy. Just lay in that tent toss and turn working up a sweat. Man you talking about being strong, sweat and the repellant mixed, aw man." He lifts his weiner out of the fire inspecting it. Not done to his likness he loweres it back into the flame."

"You know think I'll have a dog too." Sterling hands him a stick. Milt skewers one on and holds it over the flames.

"Well I think mine is done." Pulling his out of the fire. "Think I'll just eat it off the stick. Cook one more and that will be enough."

Milt checks his and lowers it back into the flames. "Not quite done yet."

Sterling put another one in the fire. "Milt look up into the sky."

Lookng up and around. "Sterling what is it?"

"Milt just look at all the stars up there. In clusters. Millions and billions won't hardly start the count."

"oh, yea, That sure is pretty. Looks like diamonds on a black velvet back ground. They really are popping in that dark sky. The moon done set. You know something else all those night critters have gotten silent too. It really is quiet and peaceful now. Ony noise now is Burt snoring."

"He went to sleep fast. Took another sleeping pill. Knocked him out quick."

"I reckon so." Milt looking at Sterling. "I almost asked him if he had an extra one. But guess he done took it. Well some one's gotta get up a little early."

"*Hol-hol-hold it Milt! My wei------*"

"*Wha-wha-wha whaz zat!? Burt wer'e being attacked again, wake up!* *Wake up!* Help me get those younguns out and behind the log. They are galloping fast>"

Burt sticks his head out the door looking around. "Attack! Attack!" Running to each tent rushing the scouts out of their tents, screaming. "Get down behind the logs, Get down and stay down." The scouts in their pajamas, Milt in fruit of the Loom breifs and house shoes, Burt with the boxers and house shoes lays down tight behind the two logs. Sterling staring at them with a grin almost laughing, when it dawns on him what just happened.

"What are ya'll doing. We are not under attack. Get up and get back in your tents and try to go to sleep for a while." All the scouts sobbing and sniffling in fear gets up and sets by the fire. Burt and Milt grabs a arm load apeice of drift wood and throws it on the fire."

Burt clapping and rubbing his hands together shedding sand off his hands. "Sterling what is going on out here? Can't hardly get any rest and sleep. Look, I just hope we ain't disturbed those ghosts again. You boys get back in your tents. Can't over sleep, ya'll know we have a important meeting sometime this morning."

Sterling leans back in his chair, looking at Milt and Burt. "ha, ha, ah, ah, ha, ha, ahahahahh. Burt sounded to me like you were sleeping pretty good. All that snoring. Almost raising your tent right off you. Justsnoring away, until Milt started hopping around hollering something about an attack."

Burt with arms folded, glaring at Sterling. "yes Sterling, I am forced to take a sleeping pill, to help me calm down some. Ain't every day I'm faced with being burned on the pole.

Milt with wrinkled fore head and staring at Sterling. "Well just what was it that caused you to blurt out like that?"

Pocco raised his shaking arm and hand. "Mister Sterling, you said those Indians wouldn't attack again. Was it them or something else?" Sobbing crying, while sliding his fore arm under his nose.

Sterling looks at Poco said, "Pocco as cute as you are. I would love to pick you up and comfort you with a big safety hug. But I can't the repellant on you is overwhelming, and prevents me from picking you up. It was nothing really. My hotdog caught on fire, and I was just trying to get Milt's attention, at how it all of a sudden turned to a browinsh, to blackish brazen appearance. Going to have a brazen dog instead ofa hotdog."

Looking at Milt and Burt again, he props his forehead in his right palm, shaking from side to side, then looks up at Milt and Burt. "Ha, aha, ah, ah, ha, ha, ha." Pointing his finger at Milt. "You, you thought we were under attack. Okay you scouts go back to bed for a while. There is no attack."

With a wrinkled froehead, and lips truned down, and eye brows pulled together looking at Burt, Milt explained. "Well he made it sound like we were under an attack. Then turns to face Sterling. "Sterling, it's the way you said it. *Hold it! Hold it! Look Milt!* I thought sore those rascals were after us."

"heeee, heeeeee, heeee, haaa, haaaa, pushing his stethson up, "Milt, Burt, ya'll are a little nervous and scared. Ya'll need to get some rest. Go back into your tents and lay back down for a while. Be sure your alarm clocks are to the loudest setting. They will not attack again tonight. Well tonight is almost gone. It is early morning. Now if we miss this ritual and be late, well thats another story. I wouldn't want to have a part in. It is going to be up to you two to get every one up."

Burt agrees and stumbles back to his tent. Burt begins mumbling again. 'Man it's four thirty and I ain't had much sleep. I'll be glad to get back home. Get in the shower and try to get this allful smelling concoction off me, and go to bed. In my bed. Maybe Janie hadn't got much sleep either. Me in her both get into the bed. Ain't really no sense in being out here with wild critters that want my flesh and blood. Heck for all I know they may have been on that space ship with him when they crash landed on the moon. And they came to Earth with him. Just by circumstance and of all places right here. Been knowing him and how he is for the past eight or more years. Then those Indian spirits, all they want is my hide and hair. Why can't they just sink back into their graves, or where ever it is they came from. Where is my water. Wished it had a shot of Jack Daniels, a hundred or more proof. This time take only a half of am ambien. Got to get some sleep or I won't get up by seven or seven thirty.'

'Ashooooo, ashooooo, ashoooooooo, ummmmmm, ummmmm, ummm, ashooo, ashooooo, ashoooooo.' Sterling pulls his hat down, glances at Burt's tent. "Well he sure went back to sleep fast. I heard him talking to himself about Jack and half of an ambiem. It knocked him out quick. He better not have any Jack Daniels stashed in there. Here, Milt sit down for a minute."

Sitting down in the chair and crossing his legs. "Sterling, he done took two of those ambiens and now another half. He should be out a while. Even an attack probably wouldn't wake him now. He ain't got any Jack in there. If he did he would've offered us a shot or two. While I don't drink much, I sure would a had a shot or two maybe three, who knows more. Plus I'd a took a couple of those sleeping pills myself. Just to sleep through this. Plus I really hate to cut those younguns hair off. Theres gonna be a lot of excited women when they see us."

"Milt I don't, know how or why you two got involved in cub scouts. Ya'll took on this scout leadership, knowing there was camping involved. And you two don't seem to be the camping type."

Leaning back into the chair relaxing. "Sterling, we knew there would be those times we would have to take the scouts on campouts. I guess we should be on the Hood scout reservation. It is a much safer place with tent pads. Camp fire areas are set up for safety. No wild critters after us. Nothing more that the usual deer population, squirrels, rabbits and similar wild life. But these boys wanted a different experience a real camp out, they requested. A long hike to a creek with a sandbar. So here we are out in a real wilderness. To top it off happen to be camped on a dead Indian reservation. Yes we are all scared senseless. Again the mommas are really going to be upset when they see their little campers, with new hairdoos. We hope you will get us through this. Hey that hand okay?"

Setting up on the edge of his chair holding his hand into the dimming fire light. "Well, I do feel a bit feverish and faint. maybe I just need to go into my tent and lay down. Get a little sleep, remember we have a big day coming up. You need to get back to bed too. It'll be day light real soon."

"Yes I know it, if this was a working day I'd already be a the plant. Reckon we might need some more repellant just to be on the safe side?"

"Not really Milt, just bed down and go to sleep."

Sterling stands up pulling his hat off. "I'm turning in for a while." Then turns to walk to his tent. "Sterling."

He turns back around, "Yes?"

"How can I? Those sleeping pills has knocked Burt out cold. He's snoring so loud, he could raise the dead. *Gosh!* Hope not. Don't need this sandbar crawling with dead Indians, and what all else."

"Milt just lay down and close your eyes. See you around seven thirty."

With the rising sun, most every one is up. Burt and Milt are helping with breakfast cooking. Burt ordered softly. "Albert you and Edward, see if Sterling is still in his tent. If so gently wake him. Tell em breakfast is getting done."

The two scouts slips toward the tent where their fearless leader is sleeping. Peeking in, Scout Albert said softly. 'Mister Sterling, Mister Sterling, Mister Sterling."

Sterling rolls over to face them. "What are you two doing up?"

Scout Edward said, But Mister Sterling sir, it is time to get up. We just about got breakfast done. Mister Foxx and Mister Hare, wants you to get up too. How is your hand?"

Sterling reaches over grabbing his hat and sets up. "What about my hand?

Scout Edward reminds him. "That hand you had to sew up last night."

Sterling trying to get his senses up and going quickly said. "Oh that, see I think it is better already. Didin't hardly notice it. Not swollen, or falling off. Just a little bit sore. I'll be on out to breakfast in a minute."

The scouts returns to their cooking chores. Sterling lays down for a minute just about to drift off to sleep. 'Hey better get up and get out there to them. Ain't no telling what they are doing. Swaggering out of his tent and stumbling in the loose sand, while tightening his gun belt, then turns back to his tent grabbing the shotgun. The sent of bacon and sausage sizzling in a large iron skillet, floats on a soft warm breeze awakens his senses for the day. Well until they can get home anyway. By the camp fire the scouts have their four burnner Coleman stove set up, and cooking. Sterling studies the group then said, "good morning. Every one sleep well?" While proping the unloaded shotgun on a log.

Scout Pocco said, "it was just like you said, right after we thought we were being attacked again I finally couldn't help but close my eyes and just like that its daylight and sun coming up. How would you have your eggs?" We have grits in this pot and toast over on the table."

Sterling looks at Milt and Burt, then pulls his stethson down. "What about you two, get some sleep and rest?"

The light breeze shifts around coming in off the creek, mixing the sent of the wilderness and creek water with that of the breakfast. Stirring in Milts hair ruffling it. Milt said, "It must ev been close to daylight before I went to sleep. I thought that swamp gnat was trying to make a fly by at us. I could a swore I heard that thing circle our camp. Once maybe twice, but then things got really quiet. Right then I figured your repellant is strong enought to ward that thing off. You sure do know how to secure a campsite."

"Pushing his stethson up. "Yep Milt, I told ya'll if you follow my instructions, you'd be all right. I sure hope the scouts have learned a thing or two." Then Sterling notices Burt kind of turning pale. "Aw come on Burt, there ain't no wild creature out here that would want any of ya'll. Ya'll are so strong and reeking of sweat and repellant. I'm just wondering what is going to happen should we reach our out post, just before going home."

Burt staring at Sterling. "Im worried about a couple of hours from now. You sure they will hold to the agreement?"

Scout Milt Junior announced. "Breakfast is ready. Mister Sterling you can go first. Hope you are hungry."

Sterling looks aroud at Milt Junior. "Why, sure I am. I am ready to eat. Where does the chow line start."

Scout Milt Junior said, "right here, here is the plates and food is right there on the table."

Sterling bends down to Milt Junior in his little greenish blue eyes and ruffled hair. "You know what? Ya'll sure are doing a good job. Why right now I'd have to vote to give each of you your camping badge. No matter what happens later."

Burt calling Sterling's attention back. "Okay Sterling I was just thinking about later this morning. Just hope we can get by those Indian ghosts and get home safely. I really need a hot, hot shower. This repellant seems to have gotten stronger over night. Hey breakfask sure smells good."

Sterling starts to pat Burt on his back shoulders but stops quickly. "Thats it Burt, get into the camping spirit. You may want to do this again sometime. After breakfast ya'll can go for a swim or fish a while. Oh and one other thing I want to show ya'll. Look at those two logs that protected each of you."

Burt wrinkles his forehead pulling brown eye brows together with a slight frown on his long face. "What do you mean?"

Sterling pulls the stethson down, as he pours a cup of coffee in the tin cup, and walks closer to the logs. Pointing at hundres of holes made by wood peckers and insects over many years. Just look at all those holes in these two logs. Those Indian Spirits sure was shooting at ya'll. Look at all those bullet holes. Some even come close to penetrating all the way through. Sure ain't none of ya'll have a bullet hole or two in ye?" They are inspecting the holes and Scouts Johnny and Roy begins sobbing and crying, as they all look surpised at the logs.

Mit stepts over to them putting a comforting arm around the two scouts. "Now, now, now. No one got hit or killed. Sterling that really bullet holes? I thought Indians had bow and arrows."

Sterling pushes his hat up sitting down on the log. Siiiiiiiiip, siiiiiiiiiip, "coffe hot and strong. Just the way I like it. Don't ya'll ever watch any westerns on television?"

While they are nodding up and down, Burt said. "Well I like to watch Gun Smoke, Bonanza and some of those Clint Eastwood westerns, and probably every one out here does too."

Sterling informed, "Then you should know most Indians carry rifles. They use bow and arrows for short range and sneak attacks. When things heat up they pull out the guns. Aw ya'll come on, don't tell me you don't know about the conspiracy of the U. S. Calvary, secretly trading guns to the Indians for goods such as buffalo hides and authentic Indian hand made blankets, made from hides of other small critters. Now lets eat, I'm hungry."

Scout Edward raising his hand, "Mister Sterling."

Sterling acknowledges, "Yes? Scout Edward."

Scout Edward asks. "What are you going to do while we are out swmming? Um reckon you could go and talk with those Indian ghosts, and see if they will just let us walk silently on by, without them having to to do anything?"

Looking intently at him with his hat pulled down low over his eyes. "Well Scout Edward what is agreed on is in blood and I can't do or say anything. So if ya'll want to play in the creek then start cleaning this camp site up. Take your tents down properly, an place them over there by mine. Then for an hour and a half ya'll can go down to the creek and play in it. I don't think there will be the historical massacure on the sandbar of Bayou Pierrie creek." Looking down the sandbar to a point where the creek cuts it into. Think I'll go right down there and pan for gold."

Scout Edward's face brightens, as his eyes get wider. "You mean, you mean, there is gold in this creek?"

Kneeling down in front of the little Scout, Sterling pushes his hat up. "You know Scout Edward, no telling what one might find in a place like this. You'll never know until you've searched. Might be surprised what you may find."

Milt interrupting, "Sterling, you mean there could actually be gold buried here?"

Sterling lifts his gaze up at Milt, then notices Burt rolling his eyes up into his head and said. "Aw come on Milt. Sterling you've got to be kidding. Who ever heard of such. Gold here in this creek."

Sterling rises up, pulling the stethson down low, staring at Burt. "Now look are we going to eat or stand here yapping. I'm hungry and ready to get packed up." Walking over to where the Scouts had plates stacked on one of the camp chairs, Sterling picks one up. Then walks to the table and loads his plate down, with bacon, sausage, eggs, grits and toast. Sitting down in his chair, taking a bite of bacon and toast. "Um Burt, you know good-n-well, if I was to find a gold nugget, maybe a solid bar, today or sometime in the future, it would start a gold rush. You and Milt would be the first ones out here."

After breakfast, Sterling said. "Oops, Milt You and Burt must be forgetting an important act."

Burt asks, "What is that Sterling?"

Sterling reminds them. "Well ya'll didn't do roll call. What if one or two of those Indian braves sneaked in and nabbed a couple of these troops. Probably don't even have roll here with ya'll. Then I think we were to say the Scout Motto and the pledge of alliegence to the flag. Even though we don't have one here with us. So before we do anything else we need to get that back in the program. No need to call roll I done checked on that.

After breafask clean up detail, every one meet out there at that tall post I have set up right over there."

Milt said, "I was wondering what you were doing after we all done settled down for the morning."

Sterling said as he picked up his chair letting it fold. Then grabbing his shotgun. "Be out there in about fifteen minutes." He staggers through the bright white sand for fifty yards from the camp and sits down a few feet from the pole. 'Whew, that smell is about to get to me. Get some fresh air for a minute or two.' After clean up, and all their camping gear is packed and ready for transport they march in single file to Sterling. "okay Milt you and Burt stand right here by me. Now just imagine the United States flag is waving tall and proud in this breeze of freedom. Ya'll call attention then salute and say the pledge. Then the Scout motto." Sterling takes his place in line beside the scouts.

Milt and Burt at the same time calls. *"Attention! Salute! Pledge!"*

We all in unison. *"I pledge alligence to the flag of the United States, of America and to the republic for which it stands. One nation under God, with liberty and Justice for all."*

"Now", Milt said. "The scouts Motto".

Then in unison. *"Always be prepared."*

Sterling said, "Allright we have things back in order? Camp clean up operation successfully accomplished?"

The scouts in unison shouted. "Yes sir."

Sterling, putting his hat back on adjusting it up and down settles it low and focused. Looking at his watch. "It is eight thirty. Ya'll have a hour and a half. Troops and leaders, You are dismissed. When ya'll hear me make the owl call, that is the signal to return to camp and change into your uniforms for the march out. *Company dismissed."* They all race down to the creek. Sterling walks, staggering in the loose sand, to his camp and packs up his. He leaves the shotgun laying across the packed tent sleeping bag, bed pad and folded chairs. He walks down the sandbar in the shifting sand to the point where the creek cuts across it. He kneels down by the swift shallow water and dips the pan into the sandy rocky bottom. Bringing it up swooshing the sand around until it shifts out. Then dips it into the creek bed again. Lifting it out, with an over flowing of sand water and gravel, he glances up to check on every one. He notices Milt, watching him. In the bottom of the pan lays a couple of small round white rocks. Holding the rocks up in the sun light as if inspecting them. He notices Scout Johnny coming toward him. He slips them into his front pocket. Milt pokes Burt on his shoulder getting his attention. Pointing at Sterling. "Burt, Sterling found something. He put it in his pocket. I'm going to find out what it is."

Burt said, "wait a sec, lets don't let him see us watching."

"Maybe he didn't see us. I think he was watching Johnny walking to him."

"Just hold tight and see what happens. I wonder what he is telling scout Johnny."

Scout Johnny kneels beside him. "Mister Sterling, you found any thing yet?"

Sterling answers. "Sure have scout Johnny." As he slide his hand into his pocket and pulls out the rocks. "nothing but a couple of white rocks. Pretty and round. Go nicely in my rock collection."

Scout Johnny inspecting them. "They sure are white and shiny."

Sterling puts them back in his pocket as Milt and Burt are looking intently at them. "Here Scout Johnny would you like to try a few times?"

Scout Johnny answers. "Sure would."

Sterling hands him the pan. "Now just dip it into the creek bed and pull up as much sand as you can, and shift it out.

Sterling looks back down as Johnny dips the pan in and dips up a pan full of sand. Johnny said, "nothing in this one. Can I try right over there?"

"Yes try where ever you like." As he digs the pan into the bed of the creek. The rushing water washes most of the sand out. He gently tips it sideways and gradually shifts the rest out. In the bottom of the pan lay a big marbleing rock with wavy artistic designs wrapping around it.

"Look here Mister Sterling, this is a pretty rock, what kind is it?"

Sterling glancing up at Milt and Burt taking notice thry are a few steps closer in courosity. "Wow! Johnny you have found what is commonly knowing as a agate. See how it shines so deep, when wet and those wavy lines all around it. You've foud a nice one. It'll be good to start a rock collection that you can show one day at a scout meeting. Put it in your pocket and see what else you can pan up."

Putting the rock in his pocket, he then digs the pan deeper into the creek bed. As the sad shifts out in the swift flowing water he finds a small arrow head in the pan. He picks it up, then stads up. "Wow! Yipee, yipee, yipee, look what I found again Mister Sterling. A arrow head, a real Indian arrow head. Look! it's in almost perfect shape. Can I keep it? Is it mine?"

"Why sure it's yours you found it."

Milt And Burt stumbling in the loose sand trying to run to Sterling and Johnny. Approaching them Burt shouts, "Scout Johnny, Sterling what did ya'll find?"

Milt interrupts, "Yea, I saw ya'll putting something in your pockets. Sterling the way you studied it, indicated something of importance."

Scout Johnny exclaims, 'Mister Burt! Mister Milt! I panned this arrow head. Got it on my third try. It's real pretty, see?"

Sterling slowly stands pulling his stethson down. With a cold blank squint eyed stare, putting his arms and hands out to his side. Then places his right hand on the sixgun with thumb resting on it's hammer. Then looks back to the camp site and toward the road out. Then side steps a few feet toward the camp. All the scouts are gathered around as he looks Milt and Burt up and down. In a low growling raspy style. "I told ya'll there was Indians out here. That arrow head proves it. It probably belonged to one of those Indian spirits when they were alive and well." The whole scout troop has congregated on the edge of the sandbar with eyes wide open and jaws gaping. "Milt, Burt I know you two are wondering what I found and tucked inside my pocket. Well it might as well be gold, as for as you know. I ain't telling. Cause if it is I'm going to find my share before letting anyone know. It'll be a ruckus sor nough. Now you scouts need to return to camp and change into your uniforms. It is almost time to go and meet with the destroyers." Then turns and walks a stumbling, slipping fast pace to his packed camping gear.

Milt and Burt dripping wet in their swim trunksand no shirts are in tow. Milt shouting. "Sterling! Sterling! What'd you mean by destroyers. I thought they were going to accept our hair."

Sterling stops, and turns around pushing his hat up. A warming breeze sweeps across the white sand bar, almost taking the stethson with it. Sterling reaches up to keep it on. "Milt, Burt there is nothing to worry about. As long as no one starts screaming, hollering, running to try a escape, the ritual will go as planned. Now get those scouts back to camp get dressed in uniforms with packs on and ready to march. I'm putting my gold pan kit back in my pack. Plus I need a coke. Gold panning makes a man thirsty."

Sterling turns back toward the camp site, Milt said. "Burt, thats it."

Burt immediately said, "What."

"Burt you know something. This is why those Indian spirits don't like us being out here on the creek."

Sterling stops and looks around. "Just what do you figure about that?"

Burt in bewiderment, wrinkling forehead, looking at Sterling. "I don't know what he is talking about."

Milt said, "Burt Sterling. Sterling you said there could be gold buried out here in the creek. I saw you put something in your pocket and you won't tell us what it is."

Burt said, "Aw come on Milton. It was probably nothing other than a couple of creek rocks. You know how he is. Just itching to start something."

Milt trying to convince Burt. "Thats what I'm saying. It is quite possible Ole western Sterling, here found a couple of gold nuggets. He is not going to let us know. Planning to eep this all to himself. Yes this could be the reason those Indian spirits don't like us being here. Not only are they guarding their mound, but the gold in this creek. Plus no telling how much could be in their mound too."

Sterling staring sliding his eyes back and fourt focusing on each one of them. Ha-----ha-----ha----hhahahahahhahahh." Throwing his head backwards, stops for a moment. Then looks at them again. "Haaa-----haaaa-----hahahhhahhhahhhaaaa. Now Milt if that was true, we'd all would a been strung up before night fall yesterday." Slidiing his hand into his pocket he reterives the two blackish gray and white pebbles, showing them in his palm. "This is what I put in my pocket. When I scooped them up they caught my attention. After examming them I figured they would fit right in my rock collection."

Burt turns his gaze to Milt. "See I told you he didn't find any gold. He done that just to get you stirred up."

Sterling looks at his watch. Placing his hand on the revolver on his side. Then stares off into the distance toward the mound. Then back down at his watch. "Okay ya'll need to call the scouts back to camp. As I ordered get them into their uniforms and ready to march. We're losing time. Sun getting higher in the sky."

Milt and Burt turns and runs stumbling in the loose sand back to the creek. In unison, they order. "Scouts! Attention! It is time to get back to camp and change into your uniforms and line up to march. And pay close attention to last minute instructions from Sterling Silver."

Milt looks at Burt. "Burt we both can't yell out orders."

"Milton! I'm also in charge here too." The scouts get out of the creek, running behind Milt and Burt as they argue.

Milt said, "as I remember, I was the one chosen to wrastle ole Strong Floating Feather, and you was going to be tied to the burn pole."

"Yea, that was cause he knew he could whup you, and then we'd all be skint and scalped."

Milt looking around. "Hey where did those younguns go?"

Burt looking toward camp. "They done went to camp and changing clothes. Lets get on up there with them. Don't want to be left out here."

"Milt wishpering, to Burt as they walk to the camp site. Burt, you know I hate to say it but, you know we may not get home. Heck with Sterling a possible space alien, we could end up somewhere else."

"Well lets just hope not and be as quiet as we can. Look Milt cut my hair as low as you can, but don't cut any skin. It ain't much there but cut what you can."

CHAPTER 7

RITE OF PASSAGE RITUAL

Sterling walks up and down the line of scouts. "Packed up and ready to march?"

the scouts, shouts in unison, *"Yes!"*

Sterling instructs, "Not so loud. We don't want them thinking we are planning an attack." Sterling fanning his face and ears fighting off mosquitos and gnats. Holding his bandaged hand up. "okay, see my hand. It is really sore now. You nor I want to do this again. Should it come down to it, Milt you and Burt will be the treaty speakers. Now here is what has to be done. Milt you will be behind me. The scouts will line up behind you and Burt brings up the rear."

Burt interrupting while rubbing the top of his head nervously. "But sterling, I don't want to bring up the rear. Actually I think Milt and I should be up front. Maybe if something happens you could have more time for rescue."

Sterling said, "Well we could do it that way."

Milt pokes him with an elbow. "That is not a good ide-----."

Sterling interrupting, "Milt, Burt, this is no time to argue. Look we will be okay as long as ya'll follow directions. Or do ya'll want to get scalped."

The scouts wide eyed tearing up, shaking their heads side to side.

Sterling walks back to the front of the line. "Okay Milt get right here behind me. You scouts line up behind Milt, Burt you in the rear. Allright, every one ready? Lets march." sterling leads them along the sandbar slipping and sliding until they reach the ancient log road leading out. When all are on the road. *"Company halt!"*

Milt wishpering, "Sterling, what is it? Something up?"

"No Milt, just giving ya'll a minute to grab your breath. When we reach the other end of that mound over there the cutting process will begin." Okay every one listen up. Right up there at the end of this mound, over there among those trees, I will give an order to stop. Every one will have to be quiet, no talking, no crying or we're gonners. Mysteriously dissappeared without a trace. Might be featured on Unsolved Mysteries. I'll have to take this arrow and dig a shallow trench down the side of the road on both sides of ya'll. This will be for the hair being harvested to fall into. Then I'll draw a dividing line across the road. I'll be standing on the other side of the line. Since I've done my ritual, I'll over see your's. Now Milt at my command you will step to this line. Do not step on it or over it. Oh almost forgot. You have to carry the feather from here. Then you will hand me the feather, and I'll hand you my bowie knife. Burt you will then walk slowly to the front, in front of Milt. Milt you will cut all of Burts hair off his left side. Thats where most of the hair seems to be. Cut it all the way down. Then turn and hand me the knife I'll hand you the feather. Then you'll change places with Burt, handing the feather off to him. Burt you'll hand me the feather and take the knife. You'll cut the lower half of Milt's left down to the skin. Leaving a portion on top hanging over the botom. On his right you'll cut the upper middle down to the skin, leaving the bottom half. Then on top left again cut a strip down the upper middle, separating the top."

Burt said. "Sterling if Milt has to cut my hair thats fine just tell him not to cut into my scalp. I don't mind giving them my hair. All of it if need be. Heck I can grow some back in a few months."

Sterling releases a slight grin, trying to remain serious. No this is not a blood ritual. Y'll cut each other like that, I'm giving ya'll over to those spirits and they'll take care of the cutting. Cut more-n-what you might think."

Scout Albert sobbing, starting a company sob. "Mister Sterling. please don't give us to those Indians. I want to get home."

Sterling reassures scout Albert. "It's okay Scout Albert. Those Indian spirits, don't want to see ya'll crying. Just listen to the rest of my instructions and ya'll will be just fine. Except for the sent of ya'll. At least we won't have to wory about that swamp gnat and hopefully not the lion either. *"Whew!"* Ya'll are one powerful force. After Burt and mIlt have successfully cut each other's hair, then scout Milt junior, will step foward. I'll hand the feather to Milt and Burt takes the knife and cuts the lower half of his hair down about half way to the scalp. Leave the top portion hanging over. Then cut a small separating strip off the top, down tto the back of his neck. Then Milt will take the knife, and Burt holds the feather. Milt will cut the opposite way. Then Milt Junior will take one stept across the line and wait. Scout Bob will then step foward and be cut in the same fashion. Yep ya'll might start a new hair fashion when or if ya'll get home. So if each one follows this procedure then no one will get captured and caged. every one ready to move foward and get it done?"

The scouts in a low voice, *"Yes."*

Sterling commands, "Troops foward march." While pulling his stethson down low in a business like fashion."

Milt, "pst, pst. Sterling looks back. Reckon you could help with the cutting of the hair. I'm so nervous about this. And those ghost indians, I just don't know if I could cut Burt's right or not. Just hope I don't cut em, he'll scream out."

"No Milt all I can do is watch and be sure ya'll do it right." Approaching the end of the mound. Sterling raises his bandaged hand up. *"Company halt!"* Steerling drags the arrow back down the road beside each one and then up the other side. Draws the dividing line a few feet in front across the road. looks off to the side of the road and nods his head foward as if in agreement. "Okay, Milt, Burt step foward. Milt hand me the feather and take this knife. Now start the cutting. All on the left side only."

Milt holding the knife, shaking nervously. Burt encourages him. "Milt little ol buddy, just do it. be careful and don't cut me. we've got to save our hides somehow. Why I can sense those Indians out there. Bows draw'd back and aimed at us." Milt finishes turns and hands the knife back to Sterling. Burt hands the feather to Sterling and Sterling passes it off to Milt and Burt takes the knifie and begins the cut on Milt.

Sterling staring off into the distance toward the creek. "Aw shoot! I was hoping this wasn't going to happen." he reaches into his pack pulling out a fresh bottle of repellant."

Milt asks, "Whats whats zat?"

Sterling holds the repellant up. "Look I think I hear that swamp gnat back there in the distance. he is a ways back but headed this way. When ya'll are through cutting you'll still have time to put this on. Just get busy. Burt begins a low squeal, grabbing at the bottle as Sterling pulls it away and grabs him. "Sh, sh, Sh. Be quiet Burt, and just get on with the cutting."

Milt said. "Burt, just cut this stuff off before that thing gets into striking range."

Burt begins the cut, and nicks Milt on the side of his head.

Milt ducks down instantly "What are you doing Burt? You cut me."

"Milt I'm sorry I can-can-can't help it we've got to hurry. Now stand back up and let me get it done. I'll try not to cut you again." Burt starts the cutting again and lets the knife slip under his shaking hand cutting Milt again.

Milt starts hopping and dancing around holding and rubbing the two wounds. "gosh dang it Burt. that stings. Sterling has he cut enough? He's gonna cut my head off."

Sterling grinning. "Look ya'll need to calm down. All the scouts are beginning to cry. Burt calm down and cut his hair right. With Milt hopping and dancing like that, is getting those braves stirred up again. They may think ya'll are doing a war dance of some kind and may attack. Now calm down and Burt get his hair cut right."

Burt looking at Sterling. "But-but-bu-but make him be still. I can't cut a moving target. Burt finally finishes Milts cut and then begins on the scouts. Milt junior gets his done Sterling hands him the bottle of repellant."

Rubs some of this on your head and neck. Milt, Burt ya'll need to get a move on. That swamp gnat seems to be circling our camp site from yesterday." After dousing himslef Milt junior tries to hand it back to Sterling. "Junior, just hold it until the next scout steps foward. Look ya'll need to save some for your leaders." With all of them cut, Milt and Burt dobs the remaining potion on themselves. With every one lined up properly, Sterling looks to the side of the road and nods as if comuting with the indian spirits. Then looks at the scouts. "ha-ha-ha-hahahahahahhhhhahhhhahhha. Well ya'll done pretty good, seems like the Indians have accepted the hair." He walks to the front of the line and commands. "Company foward march!"

About half way to the camp house road Milt begins, "pst, pst, pst."

sterlng looks back at Milt. "Sterling how bad am I bleeding? Seems like I can feel blood rolling down the side of my head."

Sterling raising his hand commands, *"Company halt!* Let me see Milt. he inspects his head without touching him. "it actually ain't bleeding much it's just sweat rolling down your head. Don't look like it needs any stitches." Then the sound of Charlene sitting at the camp house with the windows of the Surbaban down and stero turned up, reverabrates drum beats and music down through the area. Sterling exclaims. *"Listen, whats that?"*

Burt asks "What, what did you hear Sterling."

CHAPTER 8

ON TO THE FORT

Sterling said. "Just listen a minute. I thought I heard something like drums or music."

They all are looking up and around listening. Burt puts his hand up to his ear, just as the music starts again.

He points back in the direction of the mound. "There it is, I hear it. It's those Indian spirits. Cheif who ever must'ev declared not enough hair and ordered an attack on us. I know that camp road and camp house is up there somewhere. I'm gone, they ain't burning my hide."

Sterling trying to explain what they are hearing, as Burt breaks out in a dead run. Then Milt and the scouts seemingly instantly catches up with him. Sterling stands there several minutes when all of a sudden scouts Johnny and Albert runs back looking for him. Johnny said, 'Mister Sterling I'-I'm snif-snif, glad you are still here. Those Indian ghost hadn't got you yet."

Rubbing his eyes in fright and crying, "I'm, I'm so scared. I-I don't want those spirits to get me. every one just run off and left us. I don't know what we would do if you wasn't still here. I want to get home and see my mommy."

Sterling reassures them. "I can tell ya'll that no one wants any of you, much less touch ya. Not even your mommas. They may want to touch me and your leaders. So lets walk out calmly and brave." Sterling leads them, fast as he can out to the road trying to keep an eye out for left behind scouts. After studying the surrounding area, to make sure no scout is close by, they continue to walk the gravel road leading to the camp house. As they approach the camp house grounds Sterling breaks into a run. Milt, Burt, and the scouts are circling Charlene's surburban, screaming. *Charlie please open up, let us in. We are under attack. Sterling and a couple of the scouts have been captured. We've got to get outta here fast. Open up! please unlock the doors. Please."*

Charlene watching them as they run in circles around the Suburban. "Get away from my car. Now! Before I start shooting. Get back! Ya'll ain't getting in my vehicle smelling like that. get back. All right I'm gonna get the club out, ya'll don't stop."

"please Charlie, Please, get us outta here. Those spirits will be up here shortly. They're really mad. It ain't gonna be good. Please Charlie, just get us out from here!"

Sterling runs up in the middle of them "Stop it! Milt, Burt stop. There isn't any Indian spirits a coming. Ya'll can calm down now and get away from Charlene's Surburban. Ya'll are not getting in it. Now get out here.

Burt staring in disbelief at Sterling. "Sterling, you survived another attack. We thought, you, Johnny and Albert would be on poles by now. Before we topped the second hill, we thought sure ole Strong Floating Feather had gotten up in the middle of us and grabbing two or three. Especially when Milt screamed he was right behind us. All we could do was to run harder and faster."

Sterling pushing his stethson up, resting his hand on his revolver, with shotgun over his shoulder. Left leg straight and right knee bent slightly. "I know, I know. I saw ya'll's dust trail all the way up here."

Charlene gets out of her vehicle locking the doors as she shuts the driver's side. She walks to the group fanning her hands in front of her narrow face, with hair tied back. "Sterling what is wrong with this group? hahahhhhhhhhhhahhhhhhhhaaaaaaahhhhh. I was wondering what would be left of ya'll. I see now. Sterling, "while holding her hand over her mouth and fanning with the other hand. "I was standing out here looking for ya'll any minute. When I heard a thundering sound, similar to hoofs. Then a cloud of dust just below that hill, looking like smoke signals. Haaaaaaaahhhhhhhha. Then I got a whiff of a terrible sent when they topped over the hill. Looked like they were running in the air. Thought I saw daylight between their feet and the ground. By the time I rushed back to my car shut the door and locked up, they were on me.

Running in circles, trying to get in. Ya'll are not riding in my Surburban smelling like that. Man! Ya'll stink." She slips her hand down into her pocket, elbowing Sterling lightly getting his attention. Then brings her hand out. "Here Sterling, take your keys and let them ride with you. haaaaaaaaaaaaaaahahahahahhhaha." Pointing at the troops. "Whats with the hairdoos? Looks like a bunch of wild Indians got a hold of ya'll."

Burt said. "But Charlie, we are like this because you have a real wild western hero here. When he led us down to the creek, we were so far back in, it seemed as if he took us back centuries in time. The real pioneer days. Really wild Indians and beast tried to get our hides and scalps. He was the hero down there, with those ghosts Indians."

Scout Edward said, "yea Miss Charlene, he single handly fought a whole war party off us. They were shooting arrows and guns at us. Thats why Mister Sterling knew how we should set our tents up. He had us set them up in a cricle."

Charlene looks at Sterling as he stands still with stethson pulled down low. Chest poked out pridefully with hands on his chest as if pulling suspenders out, and slightly rocking back and forth on his feet. "I'll bet he did! Wow! My brave western cowboy. He was really brave huh?"

"Yes mam!" Scout Edward continued. "He was shooting at those Indians and they were shooten back at us. They circled our camp, and I could hear bullets and arrows hitting the logs we were behind. One or two arrows hit right by me. It was loud and scary. After it was over Mister Sterling had to leave, while two braves were in the bushes watching us. He had to go and smoke the peace pipe. He was gone a long time. I thought they might'ev got him. When he got back he had to sew up his hand with a fish hook and a cat whisker. Yea, he, he and all the Indians had to cut their hands and shake hands with them in blood. Wow! He is a blood brother with Indian ghosts."

Charlene exclaimes, "My goodness! Sterling did all that for ya'll. I see he has a bandage on his hand. Probably isn't much more than a scratch."

Scout Pocco with brown eyes twinkling and enlarging, "Miss Charlene he sure did, Looked just like Clint, in some of his movies, and was just a tough. Those Indians, the, they really wanted us."

Scout Edward begging for attention. "Miss Charlene, Mister Sterling said that at one time, they wanted me to sit by the cheif, with my hands and feet tied. They were going to tie Mister Burt up on a pole and surround him with fire wood. Then have Mister Milt wrastle that brave called Strong Floating Father. If Mister Milt got thrown down, the cheif was going to cut a patch of hair off me, and then have the wood around Mister Burt set on fire. Then if Mister Milt threw that brave, then the fire was going to be put out and the cheif was going to replace my hair with a feather. I was so scared. I-I-I didn't want to sit by that big ole cheif and let him cut my hair."

Charlene becoming impressed and paying close attention asked. "Well now is that so? Did Mister Milt wrastle that floating Indian?"

Scout Edward with big grayish green eyes answered. "Noooo mam. He was too scared to, and Mister Burt even fainted for a few minutes."

Milt interrupting, "Now! Now, now. Scout Edward. I was afraid I would've hurt that brave. I believe I could've thrown him several times. Good thing Mister Sterling persuaded them to change and accept his terms of the treaty. Believe me it was a lot less painful to cut our own hair."

Charlene spinning around, "Burt! Step away from my vehicle. Now no one is riding back with me. I like the new smell in it and plan to keep it as long as I can. Ya'll are not staining my new vehicle with that odor. Whew! I can't hardly stand it. Seems to be getting stronger as it gets hotter. Sterling, you know you are going to have some explaining to do. All of ye, need to be getting loaded in Sterling's pickup."

Burt walking back to the group said. "You Sterling, we thought you Albert and Johnny were gonners. Man the way they were coming after us. They were going to take us as prisioners, for some reason."

Sterling walks around the group pushing his stethson up proudly. Charlene throws her head up and rolls her eyes. "Well fellows it was like this. As fast as ya'll left there was no way any one or any thing could a caught ya'll. Well Ole Cheif Red Tail Hawk, Brave Strong Floating feather and co-cheif Sly Red Fox, galloped into view on palomino horses. A white flag waving on the end of Cheif Red Tail Hawk's spear. They galloped right up to us and pulled up to a quick stop quarting away. Cheif Red Tail Hawk dismounted his horse and the others followed him. I told Albert and Johnny not to panic and run, that they came on friendly terms. See they gave Albert and Johnny a arrow a peice plus a feather.

Cheif Red Tail Hawk spoke. "How Ole Silver, Scout Albert, Scout Johnny, you brave scouts. You Two, get sky hawk feathers. They fly higher than chicken feathers. Those making dust signals be chicken feathers. In many moons and suns, you become great peace treaty makers. Ole Silver don't speak with forked tongue. That get you scalped now. We got plenty hair for Brave Strong Floating feather and Summer deer skin."

Then I pulled out my knife.

When Cheif Red Tail Hawk saw the knife as it came out of my scabbord he instantly spoke again. Throwing his hand up. "No cut hand, hurt, sting, bleed too much. We just shake."

I said, "Hold on Cheif, it is just fitting for me to kneel down and write my initials in this dusty road. It marks this day as the great peace treaty fulfilled." Upon agreeing they too knelt down and using my knife they wrote their initials. Then we all shook hands and they walked back to their horses, head feathers up and proud, Cheif Red Tail Hawk carried his war bonnet on his hip and hung it around his horse's neck. They galloped off for a distance then stopped and turned around looking at us. Cheif Red Tail Hawk, Co-Cheif Sly Red Fox, Strong Floating Feather and Summer Deer Skin all raised their hands toward us. We waved in like manner. After one last look they turned and rode off into the forest and vanished."

Charlene looking straight up, then leaned her head toward Sterling winking a gleaming sparkling eye and smiled at him. Scouts Johnny and Albert staring at Sterling along with the rest started to speak. "Why we did-------------"

Sterling looks down at them "Sh, sh, sh." Then pulling them off to the side a short distance wishpered. "I know we didn't see any thing like this. But did you notice the look on Mister Milt's and Burt's faces along with the other boys? You two are now heros, because you had to stay with me to speak with and even shake hands with those Indian Spirits. Thats more exciting isn't it than to just say it was the music coming from Miss Charlene's vehicle."

Scout Albert said, "Yes, it sure is. *Wow!* They don't know."

"Okay lets get back in line and ready to load up on the back of my pickup. Back in line, Sterling commands. "*Attention!* Every one will get on the back of my pickup. We have survived one battle now lets see if we can withstand another. Milt, Burt the scouts are yours when you are ready give the command to load up.

Milt glances at Burt, then looks at him. "Burt I didn't mean to take the majority of the leadership on myself. You order the scouts brave and strong to load up."

"Burt's eyes light up, "Okay I am ready. Can't wait to get home and take a hot shower. I think this stuff has increased in it's power. All right. *Scouts! Load up for the trip home. Sterling! Homeward bound.*"

When they are loaded up Milt gives the signal letting Sterling know they are settled in. Charlene stands at the pickup's door bending down into the window she kisses Sterling. "Baby, I love you so much. I don't have to transport those scouts back to the hut. Hey about last night." Glancing through the back window speaking loud enough to get the leader's attention. "Um you know we also was dodging and ducking bullets too. Janie and Ann both almost got shot. Oh, well let ya'll ride into the fort proud and brave. I've already breifed the greeting party when I left. a while ago." Then she walts to her Surbaban and leads the way out.

Burt looking at Milt as he braces himself in against the frame. "See Milt I told you, they were going somewhere they shouldn't. I knew it, other men trying to capture my wife, your's and his." Pointing at Sterling. "And he ain't worried about it."

Milt yelling, BURT, I can't can't hardly hear you. Sterling is driving so fast. I just hope Ann lets me and junior in to get a shower. I think Charlene is just messing with us."

As they pass by houses, people are running out onto their porches trying to see what just passed by smelling like that. Sterling, turns onto highway fifty one in Hazlehurst and heads North to Crystal Springs. As they enter into the city limits a siren and blue lights come on. Sterling pulls over and waits, wondering. 'Wonder what I done. Wasn't speeding I know that. I stopped at the four way intersection. Well here comes the officer.'

Officer Soranise cautiously approaches the group staring at them, and the group stares back at him. He reaches into his back pocket getting his hankerchief placing it over his mouth and nose, still looking at them.

Then he bends down looking into the pickup's window. "Sterling, may I see your license?"

Sterling handing him his license, "here it is. Want to see my insurance papers too?"

"No Sterling, I know you have insurance. How long have we been knowing each other?"

"Several years, seven maybe more."

"Sterling here you are a hunter, gun and boating safety instructor, and you have a bunch of younguns and maybe a couple of adults riding in the back of your pickup. That just isn't right. What is that sent coming from them?

"Well Jamal, I took them on a camping trip last night and I think several skunks got a hold of em. Thats why they are in the back. I'm being slow and careful with em."

Here's your license back and I don't like to see this. You know the state is trying to pass a law forbidding passengers to ride in the back of a pickup. Actually I hope it passes. I tell you what. I'm gonna get in front of you and lead ya'll to the scout hut. I'm sure that is where you are heading."

"All right."

Sterling puts his license back in his wallet, Officer Soranise looks at the troops. "Hey I'm gonna lead ya'll in to the fort. Would you scouts like for me to sound the siren and keep the blue lights on?" Then he puts the hankerchief back over his mouth and nose hahahahhaahhahah.

The scouts in unison shouts, "Yes!"

He gets back into his cruiser turns the siren back on and pulls out in front of Sterling with the blue lights still flashing. driving along Georgetown Street, to the end, they turn into the scout's hut. The property is filled with mom's and dad's as they await their little brave campers. As Sterling rolls to a stop, he takes notice of all the glee and waving. Officer Sorenise, waves at the group and Sterling, shuts the siren and blue lights off and goes about on his patrol. 'Just like him to do that, leave me here alone.' The scouts are climbing out of the pickup as expressions change for all the worse on the faces of the parents. Like clouds all of a sudden obscuring the sun on a perfect sunny morning. The little boys are rushing to their parents wanting hugs and to be picked up in pride. Edward is rushing to his mother Carol, "mommy, mommy, mommy."

Carol yells. "Stop right there Edward!"

Edward stops in his tracks, dying for a hug. "But mommy I've been wanting you all night last night. A big ole Indian cheif ghost wanted me to sit by him tied up. He was going to cut my hair off while Mister Milt wrastled a warrior."

None of the parents allow their children to come any closer. The mothers are furious and crying at the sight of all the new hair doos on display. Charlene walks a few steps to Sterling. Standing to his side, and monitoring the excited crowd. "Say ain't nothing wrong with a little excitment eh? Honey I shall let you finish this camping trip. Just remember I actually think it is funny. But those mothers and fathers don't. I shall leave you with them. They may want to wrastle and scalp you. You may need to put that Stethson back on and pull it down low, so you can make some kind of peace treaty with them. I think I hear war chants coming from the crowd. See you at home, I'll have dinner cooked. I love you, my brave western hero."

"Hope I'll be home soon." He reaches into his pickup grabbing his Stethson quickly putting it on low.

Sue, Scout Johnny's mother walks to him. "Sterling! What have you done to my little boy?"

Scout Johnny interrupts, "But Mom we were att----------"

Sue putting her hand out to stop him. "John do not interrupt me. Stay right where you are utill I can figure out what to do with you."

Scout Johnny said, "But mommy I just want to tell you what happened. Mister Sterling took care of us."

"I see he really did, just look at ya. I'm holding Milton and Burt responsible for this. Well I guess I'll hear your part of it first. Um, no, no, no stay right where you are."

"Gee mom, I want to be close to you. We were attacked by some prehistoric wild cat. And then a dreadful flying swamp creature that wanted to suck our blood out of us. Yea, yea they got after us. That scent Mister Sterling had for us to put on really run that thing off. I didn't want that thing getting me. Then close to midnight a band of Indian ghosts attacked. Mister Milt and Mister Burt was in the back of our camp helping fight them off.

Milt turns his attention toward Johnny, nodding his head up and down. "Yes mam, happened just about like he said it did. But Sterling is the one who kept us protected. Those Indians was circling our camp and shooting at us."

Sue turns back staring at Sterling with beady blue eyes. Sterling standing still trying to express a tranquil, apearance while looking upwards at Sue. Trying to droop his ears to make innocence more persuasive. She demanded "Well Sterling! What about it? Why is my little boy's hair cut and gaped like that?" Looking back at her strong smelling little boy, she places hand over her mouth as tears wells up in the eyes. Then stares at Sterling and Milt, shaking her head hahah aummm um, um wa, wa, wa, wa. She shakes her head from side to side snifling then hahahahahahah wawawa." Looking back at Sterling, "why I could just about skin the three of ya'll, right now."

Sterling said as Burt sauntered closer after getting a scolding. "Mrs, Sue. Actually I didn't cut any of um's hair. Milt and Burt did." Both of them turning pale instantly. "Also they really didn't have to put that scent on themselves either. However it does repel insects really good. Bet none of them has any bites."

Maria, Poco's mother staring at her son crying, as Poco is trying to get to her for a hug and she is backing away with hands out waving. "No pocco, no, no, do not come closer. What is that smell on you? What have you done to yourself?" Puts her face in her hands crying and then fires a glaring look at Sterling, Milt and Burt.

Ann wells up in tears within her sky blue eyes, throws her long blond hair backwards, talking harsley at Milt. *"Milt, I don't, I just do not believe you and Burt would fall for such nonsense!"* Junior, even you. Well maybe I could understand you. Had I'd a known this you would've stayed home. Look! Just look at ya'll, even smell ya'll. Burt just wait until Janie sees and smells ya'll. I told her I would be glad to take you home. You better be glad you have a couple of daughters. I can't believe what I am seeing and smelling."

Wanting to hug his mother, she turns him back to Milt. Milt Junior beggiing, crying, "Snif, snif, snif, But Momma, snifsniff--------"

Ann scolding him, "don't but momma me, get back to your daddy."

"But, Momma, we were attacked by swamp creatures This scent protected us from them. Mister Sterling even fought off an Indian attack.

It was awful scary with all the shooting going on and those Indian ghosts riding cricles around us. I wished I was at home.

Milt said. "Yes dear, we are just plain lucky to come back as we are. At least we are here and safe now."

Milt Junior interrupting, "and, and Mister Sterling, had to go and smoke a peace pipe with them so we could come back home. They even wanted dad to wrastle one of the warriors, while Mister Burt would be tied up on a pole, with fire wood stacked around it. Then Edward was to be tied up by hands and feet and set by the Indian cheif. If dad got thrown by the Indian, then the wood under Mister Burt would be set on fire and the cheif would cut a bunch of hair off Edward's head. If dad threw the Indian then the fire would be put out and Edward would get a feather to replace his hair. They was gonna wrastel until one of them got knocked out. But Mister Sterling talked them out of it, because he knew dad couldn't wrastle that Indian, and so they just let us cut our hair."

Ann staring at Sterling as if saying I could just tear you to pecies. "Do what! Wrastle a Indian ghost. Aw I can't believe what I am hearing. I am just embarrassed and ashamed of you two. Sterling smoking a peace pipe with some Indian ghosts. Milton wrastling a Indian ghost, why he can't even wrastle our basset hound Rufus."

Gail, George's mother is calling her husband, while listening to Milt Junior's side of the events in disblief. "David George, you need to come over here and get George, when you leave from work. He'll be right here at the scout lodge. You'll smell why he ain't going home with me. He might have to go home with one of these leaders or that pranster, Western whats his name."

Milt talking to Ann, with an emergence on his wrinkled face, "Ann I've got to get home and take a hot steaming bath. I can't stand this smell any longer. Me and Junior will go and get our hair cut and straightened out after we get a nap. Been up bout all night trying to keep ftom getting arrowed, or eaten by some wild swamp critter. Now will you unlock the car?"

Ann about to lose her temper with dark blue eyes squinting at Milt. "Milton, I said ya'll are not getting in my car. have that new Avalon smelling worse than you two. It is staying clean and fresh. I'm the one paying for it. You two will have to get a motel room until you go broke, or get that scent off. Heck just camp out in the back yard. Ain't getting in the house and getting on the beds. Isn't happening. There is a bed and breakfast within walking distance of here. Since ya'll hiked so far back into the woods to a creek, I'm sure that little short walk won't hurt either of you. If they will accomondate ya." A musical melody comes on Ann's phone, as she digs it out of her purse. "Hello!" Looking at them in disbelief and shaking her head as tears well up. "Yes Janie they have made it back safely. Except one thing."

Janie's voice trembling a little on the phone. "What is that? Burt is alright isn't he. I've been a little worried about him since early this morning."

Ann usssssppp, taking in a deep breath. "Weeeell, Janie it seems that he and the whole outfit, was almost scalped and burned by a tribe of Indian ghosts. Janie It's bad. Believe me it's even hard to look at em. Stinking and new hair doos, that'll beat any rock-n-roll band. Actually they all smell like they slept with skunks and bears pissed on em. I can't stand this sight and smell any longer."

Other parents in disgust of Sterling and his two co-leaders, to the point of giving them to Sterling. Then quickly decide that wouldn't be the proper action to take.

David arriving on the scene jumps out of his Ford Ranger rushing to the scouts huddled up on the out skirts, stops in his tracks. "What da heck is that smell. George, get your tent and other supplies and get in the back of the pickup. I'm going to have to drown you in tomato juice. Maybe after a week or two of juice treatment it might get weak. You are on an extended camp out.

CHAPTER 9

STILL CAMPING

Ann gets into her car and drives off in a hurry. Other parents with their children speeds off in several directions and blocks, leaving Sterling, Milt, Milt junior and Burt, standing in the scout lodge's yard. Sterling looks at them a long minute. "Okay Wyatt, Doc and Billy, mount up, we'll be at the Okay Corral shortly." Entering into the neighborhood, around the circle they turn ito Burt's and Janie's drive. Burt jumps out before Sterling can stop and runs to the front door, intending to get in. While Burt is trying to get in, Janie turns into the drive, bringing her blue Nissan Sentra to a screeching halt and leaving the door open as she attacks Burt. This medium tall slender blue-green eyed long brunett haired lady in a green skirt and blouse fights Burt off the porch. "Burt stay away from this porch. Just look at you." Then turning to look at Milt and Junior. "My goodness! Ann was right. If it wasn't bears then what pissed on ya'll? I tell ya, one thing, how'd you get sprayed by skunks? Scouts are supposed to know about the wild life they may encounter in the wilderness. What'd ya'll think they were? House cats to play with? Tell me, just explain this to me. Oh thats right I bout forgot, Sterling." Staring at him turning her blue eyes into dark blue storm clouds, pointing her finger at him. "And there he is, that ole skunk and bear. Sterling what did you do to them?"

Milt Junior trys a run at her.

"Stop right there. don't come any closer."

Milt Junior begins crying, as Janie folds her right arm across her chest placing her left elbow on the hand, wrist and hand under her chin. "Miss Janie, Miss Janie, please Miss Janie, we would not be here right now if it wasn't for Mister Sterling. I was so scared I couldn't talk. I had to lay in my tent all by myself. Mister Sterling even had to cut his hand, with those Indian ghosts, after smoking a peace pipe. I saw him sew his hand up."

Janie with her face in her hands as tears well up in her eyes, shaking her head from side to side then crying turns to laughter, as she peeks at the three Amigos. Then puts her face back into her hand. Burt, Milt, and Junior waiting for what may come next. Sterling with ears drooped down and eyes turned up. Then she looks at them again, with tears and embarrassment in her face, "hahahahahah, ahaha, haha, wow! The old television western scene. The hero goes into the Indian tribe and smokes the peace pipe. Then he has to cut his hand and sew it up. Aw, come on Milt and Burt, as many times as ya'll've seen Clint Eastwood, Dean Martin and other actors do that on television. Why just look. Pointing at Sterling. "he can't even put a bandage on right. I bet its only a scratch. I just can't believe ya'll fell for this. What about those swamp creatures, a bobcat and horsefly. So ya'll had to put this stinking stuff on? Ya'll need to be getting ye, tents up. Ya'll are not coming in here."

Burt cries, "but hun, I've got to get in there and get a really hot soaking bath, and then a shower." Jan steps inside and retrieves her cordless telephone, comes back out on the little porch, as she dials Ann's number.

"Hello, oh Jan, whats going on with our braves?"

"Ann it's really getting worse, the more they sweat in this sun the stronger the scent gets. I'm afraid it is going to cause alarm in this neighborhood. I'm so embarrassed of these western cowboys, I'm heading West. I'm going to turn my store over to Carol and let her run it a couple of months. I'm taking Beth and June to my parents. They've been wanting us to come for a visit. Now is a good time to go. I'm headed to Jackson and just get any flight I can to Montana. As soon as I can get us packed we are gone."

"Well Jan I think that is what I may do too. I'm so embarrassed about this. had I a known what that ole Western Sterling had up his sleeve, little Milt would've stayed here with me. Lets see it is about one o'clock, doctor Lance Nichols had just called me back and wants me to bring Little Milt to his office now. Just tell ole Silver to drop Milt and Burt off at our home. They can camp out next to Rufus, right out side his pen. He'll need someone to feed and water him. Nichols said he thought he might could get junior clean and rosy again. Hopefully Monday Junior, Joni and I will be on a three ten to Yuma. Tell Sterling to giddy them up over here."

"Gotcha my friend," while running a stare at the four males. "I'll be glad to send them back, goodby."

Janie still staring at the three. "Okay Milt and Burt get back in Sterling's horse buggy. Sterling, Ann told me to tell you to drop Junior off at doctor Nichols office. He seems to think he can clean Junior up and ready to travel. And Rufus will need someone to feed and water him. So ya'll can camp out over there."

Burt begging and whinning, "but Honey bunch, Sugar Pie, Sweet bread. Ple, ple Ple--ase don't leave me. If doctor Nichols can get Junior clean I'm sure he can get me just as clean, and smelling fresh again."

Janie pointing a long slender fore finger at Sterling, staring at Burt. "Don't honey bunch me, ha! Any one falls for him. Just look at you Burt. I can't deal with this scent." Throwing a fiery glance at Milt, "hahahahahahahahah, Milt and Junior those are two of the most red neck mohawks I've ever seen. There probably isn't a barber within driving distance who would even think about touching your heads." Putting her face back in the hands she begins crying and shaking her head from side to side glancing up at the three amigos, then turns into laughter. "How come, ya'lls hair is long on one side and short on the other with some kind of feathering. Oh thats right the Indians told ya'll to cut that style. And what did ya'll use to get that style? Oh don't tell me, it was with stone knives. And I'll bet neither of ya'll or anyone else in the chicken feather scout gurillers saw those blood thirsty swamp creatures, much less attacking Indian warrior braves. Ya'll will have plenty of time to think about this. Since ya'll are going to camp out by Rufus a few weeks I'll leave tomorrow morning, or when ever I can get a flight. I've got to be getting packed." Then she turns entering the house, leaving him, Milt and Milt Junior standing in the yard agahst, not believing what they'd heard, then the closing of the door.

Sterling said, "Ya'll mount up and lets ride."

Sterling arrives at Doctor Nichols clinic, as Ann is driving into the little parking lot. She gets out of her Avalon, staring at Milt, then Burt and Sterling as if she could hang him. "Come on Milt Junior, we're going to try to get you clean, and be ready to travel tomorrow. We are spending the night with Janie. All our luggage is packed and ready to go." Firing a fiery arrow of a stare back at Milt. "And should you get clean somehow, call me at Mom and dad's. You two need to head on over to camp Rufus. He's been fed and watered today. So ya'll can get your tents back up before night fall. I just hope Junior can be cleaned." Then she makes Milt Junior go into the doctor's clinic.

Sterling standing there in the parking lot, looking at Milt and Burt in their hopeless condition. "Okay Wyatt and Doc mount up, lets ride."

Arriving at Milt's desolate home range, they unload all their camp supplies. Sterling helps them set the tents up and makes sure Rufus can't get out of his pen and run off too. Milt asks, "aren't you going to set your's up and stay with us?"

Sterling replies, "no way, I'm going home. For now, ya'll have plenty of hotdogs and chips. Plus a a few cokes still in the ice chests. I'll come over in a couple of days and check on ya'll. If you want water there is the facuet right over there. Just don't get wet. Maybe in a few days of this hot dry weather the scent will dry into a powdery residue and then you can scrape it off with your knives. Ya'll don't need to build a fire, there is plenty of street lights lighting this neighbor hood well camp hood up."

Sterling gets back in his pickup and backs out the drive waving at them. "I'll be here Monday afternoon to check on you guys." Sterling speeds off down the street.

Milt said. "Well Burt, we've got to call Sanderson farms and request a couple of month's leave."

Burt said whinning and crying, "waaaaa----waaaaaaaa-wwawwawwawaaa snif-snif, hak, hok, hunk, I good -n-well know that. We'll have to drive to the plant and try to talk with Peterson about it. You know how he is, wants to know every little detail of why we need the time off."

"Well, um Burt I'm quite sure if they don't believe us they can smell why."

Sniff, snif, snif, and we won't be getting paid either. Just look at me, And even smell, it's like I'm rotten or something. It is just embarrassing to be in the billing and purchasing department and allow myself to be done like this."

"Yea, yea and Sterling gets out of this smelling like a rose. He can go back to that Kuhlman plant fresh and clean. Like he never went on an overnight camp out."

"Plus we'll probably be relieved of our scout leadership too. I just hope those kids are alright. At least they don't have to go to school Monday. We'll just have to wait and hope we can get approved for the time off. I know they aren't going to allow us to return like this. Sniff, snif-snif, wa-aa-aaaaaaa waaaaa-----aaawaawaawaaaa."

Sterling arrives home and entering the house, "I'm hooooo-----mmmm-eeeee."

Charlene walks to the living roon greeting him with a kiss. "Hahahahahahahah, Honey I missed you last night, when I walked in from our little outing. It just didn't feel right going to bed alone. I was really, really worried about you being tied up on the Bayou Pierrie creek Indian mound. How are your two buddies doing?"

Sterling hugging and holding Charlene, "Well, I think they will be alright for a day or two. I'll give em a week to figure out they will have to go to doctor Nichols. Unless they figure it out sooner. I'll see that they are fed and watered, hahahahahah. Hey what ya got cooking?"

"I'm cooking hamburger and fries. I thought you'd be hungry when you got here. You can go and get in the shower while I finish up. Get to smelling rosy again honey. We may have some pow wowing and wrastling later too."

"Hey, hey, I'm all for that, I'm gone to the shower." He kisses her and heads to the bathroom."

After dinner, Sterling walks to the living room and sets back in his recliner to watch the news, while Charlene finishes the dishes. She prances into the living room takes the remote turnning the television off.

"What are you doing?"

She puts her finger in front of her lips lets out, "shh", then points a finger at him while dancing her way to the tape deck. Popping a classical music cassett tape into the player, waiting for the music to come on. She turns to Sterling while opening the top of her blue blouse a couple of buttons down. Slowly saunters to him swaying from side to side as he watches her. She sits down in the recliner laying half way on him. The sweet scent of his millionaire colonge stirs her senses as she puts a hand on his chest. He puts his arm across her hips as she leans onto him pressing her red lips onto his for a long kiss. He then slides his hand up her hips as she squirms down closer to him. They break their kiss as another song raffles through the room. Sterling lifts her up, unbuttoning her shirt revealing only what he is to see. Then starts kissing her neck close to her ears

"Oooo baby, you are getting me turned on and hot. "hahahaaaaaahaaaaahaahaaa I want you." His kisses and licks up and down her neck and behind her ears bringing a chilling tickle. With a romaning hand up inside her blouse, she rolls over onto him, kissing again. Then she raises up pulling his shirt off revealing a narrow but muscular hard chest. Sterling slides her blouse off when she stands up shaking a brazened face throwing her long reddish brown hair back, swaying and motioning at Sterling. He rises up embracing her. "I love you baby."

"I love you too my man, Wild Western Sterling Silver." He then reaches down picking her hundred pounds, maybe a little more up, as she wraps her arms around his neck laying her head on his shoulder. Entering the bedroom he lays her down on the bed. He leans down to kiss her, noticing how her hair is spread over the area, and the diamond ear rings sparkle in the dim light of the bed side lamp. Bending down over her pressing his lips onto her red hot lips and slowly sildes his wandering hand over her body.

Breaking the kiss, With a deep sigh, "love me Sterling, I'm yours. I want you baby.

Five am she wakes up. Sterling is wrapped around her as she lays there, thinking how good and comfortable to be laying in his arms, and sunggles in closer for a few moments. Then gets up and showers. Then puts a pot of coffee on. Sitting at the table sipping a steaming cup of coffee, and breathes a prayer, for the day's worship service. Then gets up walks back to the coffee refilling her cup and starts cooking breakfast. The sizzle and smoky sent of bacon in an iron skillet awakens Sterling. he lays there a minute and gets up, wanders into the kitchen.

"Good morning, Baby I was just fixing to come and wake you. Sit down and have a cup of coffee, while I finish breakfast. How do you want your eggs? Oh don't tell me cooked hahahahah, beat ya to it. Guess what I already beat ya to it. They have the whites white and yellers yeller" as she places his plate on the table." Taking his cup, "I'll refill it."

"Don't forget the three spoons of sugar. hahah."

She returns the cup and then sets her plate down. Pulling the chair out enough to set in.

After eating he rises up, wiping his hands and mouth, "thank you baby I really enjoyed the breakfast. How about just putting the dishes in the sink with hot water, and I'll take care of them after we return from church."

"Okay honey, all I've got to do is get my self dressed up nice in pretty, and start smelling good-n-sweet. I'm going to head on down to the church. Mrs. Rose wants me to go over her song with her one more time. I keep encouraging her that she is gonna do good. So I'm going to help her. She really has a nice singing voice if she would just come on out with it. So I'll see you later at the church my man, I so much love you."

"I love you too baby, I'm going to the shower and get dressed and come on down. Go over the Sunday School lesson one more time."

"I'll see you in Sunday School." While opening the bedroom door and enters in. putting her black mid length skirt, red pinstriped blouse on, then steps into her black higheel shoes, fastening the straps and swings the light pink ladies blazer around wiggling her arms into it. Stares one last look in the mirror fluffing her hair. Sterling is just about ready, and sitting at the table with another cup of coffee, when she emerges from the bedroom. "Wow Charlene, you are bueatiful."

As she spins around smiling, "thank you baby, I've got to be headed out. Mrs. Rose is probably waiting for me now, even though its still a little early. I'll see you later, "Hey you gonna be looking good too. Finish dressing and come on down."

Sterling finishes the Sunday School lesson a few minutes early, so three of the day's ushers can get out to the entrance doors and start greeting people as they come in. As they exit the room Charlene hugs and kisses him on the cheek. "That was a good lesson. Hey you are looking great today. I may call on you in a few minutes."

"Thank you baby. You know when I chinced this red tie up on the collar of this white shirt, I couldn't help but to grab the bottom of my chin, shaking it and said as I peered into the mirror. Why you good looking rascal you. Then the mirror reached out and kissed me."

"Remember Sterling you're in church right now, don't forget that. hahahah. I've got to get on to the choir room."

"Tell Rose she is gonna sing great because I prayed for her."

Entering into the santuary with the usual greets, he sits down on the front pew along the side of the piano. Charlene's parents enters and sits down beside Sterling. Sterling looks at them in surprise and then hugs her mother and shakes hands with her father.

"How you been doing Sterling?" as Charlene leads the choir out as the musicans take their places at the organ and piano. Her eyes brighten in surprise as she sees her parents sitting with Sterling. Standing at the pulpit she declares. "lets all stand and sing the doxology." When the music starts, the pastor and deacons enter as she leads the song. As the music fades at the end she declares, "praise the Lord, praise the Lord, All you people praise and worship him. King of Kings, Lord of Lords, For he is worthy. Worthy is the Lamb. Lets worship him in Jesus name. For I love my Lord and saviour Jesus Christ, all glory to be given to him. A-men. Please remain standing as Brother Stockon leads us in the invocation prayer."

As he rises from his chair approaching the pulpit he decalres, A-men Sister Silver," looking at her, "I love the Lord to, then turns to the congregation and says, "Lets pray." And in the name of Jesus Christ our Lord and Saviour a-men. Come and lead us in our musical worship Sister Silver."

She returns to the pulpit, motioning the audience to sit down, while keeping the choir standing. Looking over the congregation she says. This opening song of worship isn't in the hymnal, but on a sheet of paper in the pew rack. Please get it and follow along singing out. And I would love to give a great welcome to my parents, Reverend Charles and Carol Wright, from a small community in Alabama, and pastor of the First Baptist church of----------. Glad to see you mom and dad, welcome. Now Sterling be watching me and pay attention. Looking back over the congregation, "music and song open lets begin." The piano starts in a lively high pitch and the organ follows in. Charlene begins a small clapping, and then directs the song. In high key note.

"Let the music p---la---y, let the music pla--la-y ohoh, ohoh, sing unto the Loooo-rr--d sing unto him praises. Let eh mus----i--c, pla--y--, o let the mu----si----c play." Then she starts swaying and clapping to the rythym sliding from side to side getting the choir swaying and clapping. Then sways back to the pulpit. "Ohhh sin---g unto him, sing for his love end---ur--rs for----ev---er, his lo---ve en---dur--rs for-ever. Let the music pl--ay." Then motionig for Carol to come up and help her. The aging white haired short lean lady comes up beside her. She then takes the lead and says. "Come on ya'll lets sing and play unto the Lord. Let the mus---ic play, ooo-hhhh ooooooooo let the mus-----ic play. For he is alive, he is alive, sing praises unto him leee----tttt the mus----ic let the music-----pla---yyyyy.

They and the choir are clapping and swaying. Charlene takes the lead, "Oooooooo-----hhhhhh. let the mu----sic pl---ay, oh let the mu----sic let the mus---i-c p---lay. Ohhh I will sing, I will sing of my re---dem--er and his love. Ohhh let the mus---ic-- let the mu----sic pl--ay, let the mu---sic pla---y. And his woun------der---ous lo---ve for me. Le th---e Mus-------ic---c pla---y, ohohoho, let, le---t th---mu---s----ic pl-----ay."

Carol takes the lead again motioning for the audience to stand with upraised arms and bobbing and clapping with the mic in her hand. "Let the mu----sic play, let the mu---s---ic pl----ay, Ohhhhhh let the mu---s--ic pl---ay, I stand amazed in the presence, ohh---ooo let the musi----c pl--ay Let the music play."

As they slow down to the end and allowing the musicans to play one last verse. The music softly fading charlene sings quietly, "let the mus----ic pl--------a---------y."

"Thank you mom for helping with this bueatiful lively song. I was going to call on Sterling, until I saw you out there. This dear mom has been in the music ministry for as long as I can remember. Mom and Dad I love ya'll. Okay, now remain standing for the next hym. Turn to hymn number four eithty eighty. The Lily of the Valley. Shortly Mrs. Rose Henderson is coming to sing about that lily. So remain standing and lets sing out." Then looks at the painist and organist as she begins directing. At the end, "I'm going to ask my dear husband Sterling to have prayer with us now."

At the end of the offertory Charlene directs the choir to come down, as she takes her seat by Sterling, wiggling down between him and her dad. She reaches over and hugs him and then leans into Sterling, as he puts his arm across her shoulders while resting it on the top of the pew. Rose walks up to the pulpit at the end of the offertory hymn, looking at Charlene for confidence. Charlene gives her a thumbs up smiling, folding her hands together in prayer. Rose motions the pianist to start and she sings "Hes my lily in the Valley."

At the end of the service and invitation, Reverend Stockon said. "I am pleased to welcome Reverend Charles Wright and his wife, the parents of Sister Silver. I will ask him to pray our closing prayer, and remember. Enter to worship, depart to serve."

"A-men and a-men dear Lord." The painist and organist begins the song. "Let the music play." Charlene walks briskly to Rose. "Mrs. Rose, you did a fantistic job on that song. I'm so proud of you."

"Thank you Sister Silver, you helped make it happen. I really enjoyed being up there."

"I'm glad you did, and remember to give the glory and honor to the Lord, acknowledging him in all things. You really sounded wonderful Sister. Just let me know any time you'd like to sing again."

As Gerald Henderson arrives, "Charlene again thank you."

"Well Gerald what did you think of the song."

With a deep base voice the large short haired man said. "You did great honey. I am really proud of you. Hey want to go to Cracker Barrel in Pearl?"

Reverend Charles turns to Sterling. Sterile, my favorite Son-in-Law, what ya' been up to strile hahahahahah."

Carol corrects him. "Charles, it is Sterling, and you only have two Son-In-Laws, and both are your favorites." She then rolls her eyes up.

Sterling said. "Charlene baby," As she arrives back, "are we going to knues again today?"

"Sure we can," she answers," I was hoping we would."

"Allright!" Sterling exclaims. "Since its Sunday I'll have a plate of fried chicken."

Charles looks at Sterling, "haahahahahah, ain't you funny. That was a good one Sterile"

Carol rolls her eyes up again, Looking at Charlene. "I guess the saying is true women ends up with husbands similar to their dad's. Just look at those two. Both of ya'll are just comedians."

"Mom just ride with me to Knues. Dad and sterling oh, I mean Conway and Knotts, can ride together."

Carol said, "come on Charlene, lets go and let them follow us."

Charlene said. "I'm sure if they fall behind and get turned around, maybe one of them can eventually find their way to the resturant." Then she comes up to Sterling and gives him a quick kiss. "I'll see you there my man. Don't let dad out do you. Lets go."

Walking out of the resturant, Sterling pokes Reverend Charles in his side, "man that was some really good fried chicken, and catfish."

Reverend Charles said, "I actually liked the catfish better. Ate so much I feel I could swim across the Mississipi."

"Dad, how bout getting in my Suburban and let mom get with Sterling? I need to spend a few moments with both of you, plus one on one time like we used to. Especially when we went out shooting."

The tall white haired man with a narrow face and dark brown eyes, Charles said. "Sure I can trust Sterling with your mother."

"But Dad, can you and I trust mom with Sterling? hahahahahahahaha" they both break out in laughter at the thought. Looking at her dad smiling as she notices his salt and pepper hair with a heavy dose of acqua velva steaming off his neck and face. She leans over a second when clearing the intersection, sniffing. "Dad are you sure you have enough of the Acqua Velva on?"

"Well I hope I do. "No telling who might get a wiff of ya. Gotta have a great impression out in front of ya. Remember I've always taught that to you and Amanda."

"Yes, Dad, I remember, but that much of an impression? You know sometimes I see and smell a resemblance between you and Sterling. Dad I'm so glad you and Mom surprised us with a appearance. Y'all going to spend tonight with us?"

"Uh, wish we could, but we'll have to get on back home shortly. It's about a three and a half hour or so drive. I told a couple I would be at the hospital with them tomorrow morning. His wife is going in for a cancer biospy. I've got to shepherd the flock. You do the same here don't you?"

"I make it my utmost importance. This morning when you heard the lady sing the special, I had been working with her several weeks on that song."

"well I can see you are a great mentor. Plus under better situations than mine."

Almost home home, Sterling saying, "Mom, you and Dad going to spend tonight with us?"

"No, we will have to go back later this afternoon."

"well ya'll going to go back to church with us? I think Charlene is going to sing tonight."

"Won't be here that long. Charles has to be back home. Got to be at the hospital for a middle age couple who may have to go into a fight with cancer. She has a biospy scheduled for tomorrow morning and they want him to be there. You know Charles, he is going to be there. I probably will go with him. It is a scary time in their lives."

Taking her eyes off the road, for a moment looking at Sterling. "Sterling, tell me something."

"If I can, I will." Offering a puzzled look at her.

Glancing back to the road then back to Sterling. "I'm worried a little about Charlene. Is she doing allright? I mean with those head aches she has."

"Well, as far as I know she doesn't seem to have them as often. Doctor Bellows has got her medications right. But he is conducting more indepth blood work on her. We'll find out the results in mid July."

After a couple of cups of coffee and cake they walk out with Reverend Charles and Carol. Hugging and saying byes the older couple backs out the drive. When they turn up the road, they are waving at them. Sterling and Charlene stands in the drive watching as they drive off into the distance. Charlene turns to Sterling. They hug and hold each other a few minutes. Sterling I'm so glad we met. I know God had you reserved for me. With mom and dad surprising us with a visit and then leave so soon it brings a sense of loneliness. But I can look at you and it just melts away. Hey baby you know I'm singing tonight?"

"I thought I heard you telling mom that you are."

"I'm singing a couple. Rose and I are going to do a duet in the near future."

"That'll be good. That song you and mom lead this morning, I really liked that one, and you two done a supurb job on it too."

"Thank you baby." They walk back inside, closing the door behind him, while Charlene picks up the cups taking them to the kitchen. Hey honey, how about taking this last cup of coffee. Want it, hate to throw it out."

"yes I'll drink it, and then I'll clean those dishes up like I told you."

"Baby don't worry about that. Hey I hope Mom and Dad didn't think too much about them."

"I don't think they did. He'll probably call me tomorrow sometime and tell me to throw you off the porch."

She brings him the cup of coffee. "oh yea, it'll take you and the whole deacon body to do that. hahahah. I'm going to get freshen up and be going on back to church. Go over the songs while waitiing for the choir members to come on for practice."

A few minutes later Charlene returns to the living room, 'Sterling I'm headed back to the church. See you later my man. "I so much love you."

"I love you too, baby. I'll be on in a hour or so. See you there."

She backs out the drive. Sterling gets the kitchen cleaned up spic and span, then freshens himself up and goes to the church.

3:00 am buzz, buzz, buzz, Sterling rolls over reaching for the alarm, looking at the glowing dial to be sure the time is right. Then lays back down closing his eyes. Buzz, buzz, reaching for the clock again turning it off. Then sets up on the side of the bed a minute. It is back to work again. Wished I could be off all the time like last week. Then stands up and walks to the bathroom. After getting dressed he makes a couple of cups of coffee and sets down at the table waiting for the brew to finish. He pours a cup of coffee and walks back to the table sitting down he bows in prayer a few minutes. Then opens his Bible to the book he has been reading and studing. After a quick breakfast of toast and sausage he cleans up after himself then returns to the bathroom. He brushes his teeth and then shaves, doushing himself with English Leather after shave. Well it is time to get up the highway to work. Making one last check on Charlene, he slips out the door, locking it behind him.

Milt and Burt drives to the guard house at Sanderson Farms. The guard, Daniel comes out from the shack to check their badges. "Whoa, Mista Hare and Mista Foxx, you twos ain't getting any closter. What'd ya roll in over tha weekend? Scent woorse than maw dog Henny when he finds something ta roll in. Why didn't ya'll take a shawr, before coms to work?"

Burt leans out the window of his Powerwagen, "Daniel, call Stan Peterson out here. He should be in his office."

Milton opens the door and gets out. Daniel a strong, tall black man, with a muscular body, spots Milton, and steps farther out of the guard shack, as far as the springy, coiled phone line allows. "Mista Foxx, don't come any closter. Ins fact gets back in that truck. Mista, Peterson, um, youse ain't gonna believe who I's a looking ats and smelling. Thats whys dey didn't comes to the plant on time. Jest gets out yere before-n I runs, em off. Whew, dos they smell."

"Hold on Daniel, I'll be right on out."

"Mista Hare please moves that truck backs, away from yhere. Mista peterson is um on his way outta yhere."

Five minutes Stan Peterson walks briskly, with outstretced long slender legs, in a business fashion to the guard house. "Daniel, what is going on with these two men?"

"Mista Peterson, I thinks maybe yos might ought to go out thar ans smells for yoself. I thanks maybe they needs some times away from yhere."

Stan walks out to them. The two men start to get out of the pickup. "Hey ya'll get back inside. What on earth have ya'll been rolling in?" Fanning himself with his hands.

Burt answered. "It is a rather long story, Stan. You know Sterling."

"Yes I know Sterling. You two done let him talk ya'll into something. Why I just can't believe you two. And I know ya'll need some time off. Milt, I'm going to let Tom supervise your department for a couple of weeks. Um Burt I'm requiring you to stay in contact by phone with your clients every day. Yes I knew what ya'll were going to ask when Daniel called me. Nope, No, I'm giving you two only one week. With two weeks unless you request vacation time you'll file for unemployment benefits. So what do ya'll want one week or two on vacation time?

Burt answers "I'll request two weeks vacation, because I don't have any way to contact my clients list."

Milt said, "I'll second that, I want two weeks too. That'll still leave me one week."

Stan staring at them from a distance said. "All right I'm going to approve it when I get back to my office. You two had better be clean and fresh when ya'll come back in two weeks. Get that pickup started and get out of here. What in the world ya'll let Ole Silver talk you into I don't know. But get clean. Two weeks be clean when you come back here." Then he walks back to Daniel. "You done a good job. Two weeks from today they are suppose to come back to work. If they aren't clean don't let'em get by. Call me out again."

Daniel said. "Sos will boss."

Heading back to their home range, Burt suggests "Milt how about lets stop and McDonalds, for a sausage and bisquit. I'm a little hungry. I'll buy."

"Hey that sounds good to me. Sure would love to go in and sit down with a good cup of hot coffee. But I doubt we can. They'll run us out. You know ole Peterson was quite willing to give us some vacation time."

"Of course, we only have three weeks and right now is a good time for the chicken industry to allow vacation time. It was easy for him to cheat us this way. He knew what he was doing. Now we're down to only one week. Yep I was planning to get back into deer hunting a little. But not with Sterling."

Pulling into the drive through, "hey Milt how about a sausage in gravy dish and coffee."

"yea, thats good."

"We'll just drive over to the Wal-Mart parking lot and eat. Doctor Nichlson is probably open by now. How about lets stop by and ask him if he could clean us too."

"Well couldn't hurt, Burt, This stuff, whatever this is, it's about to get to me."

Arriving at the vet's office Milt notices a sign posted on his door. "Aw heck, he ain't gonna be open today. How in the world does he make a living not working. Acts like a banker. Let me go and see when he will be open." Milt returns with head hanging low, and shaking it side to side. "Burt I can't, just can't believe it. He won't be back before next Wednesday. He's gone on a long coastal fishing trip. Shoot! Summer tme fishing, winter off into the mountains deer and elk hunting."

"Well Milt lil buddy, I hate to say it but looks like another week of camping out. Can't even keep up with the news and weather reports. Heck the world could come to an end and we would'nt know it. Plus I miss Janie, Beth and June. I wonder what she is doing now."

2:30 pm, Sterling gets off work and drives to Milt's home. Getting out of his pickup, waving at Burt and Milt. "Hows things going men um scouts?"

Burt asked, "how long did you say this stuff would last?"

Sterling answers, "Just give it a few more days. Did ya'll try to go to work today?"

Burt answers. "Well we got to the plant but, we couldn't go in. Daniel called Stan out to the guard house. He said that we could have one week off without pay or two weeks vacation. So we took the two weeks. Good thing because we went by doctor Nichols office to set a time for him to try to clean us. He seems to have done a good job on those younguns."

Milt interrupting, 'Yea, yea, he must've made so much money off this that he closed up until next Wednesday. Gone sea fishing. I don't know how we will make it another week."

Urrrrrrrr----grrrr--gr------awl, grrr-----rrr---awl. Sterling looks at the dog pen. Rufus raised up on the fence staring at Sterling. "Whats his problem?"

Milt said, "We--l--l I wonder too. Everytime I try to replenish his water dish he tries to get a hold of me. I'm quite sure Sterling, it is this powerful sent. Heck, with our sweating it gets worse and worse. Practically all of the residents here have moved."

"Well I see Burt must've walked over to his house and got the pickup, so ya'll would have a way to get around."

Burt replied, "yes, we walked over there. Oh I mean hiked."

"Well I just came over to see about you. If either of you needed anything I'd go and get it."

Burt said, "Naw not right now. We are going to go over to the Sonic for a burger and fries later. Oh yes one thing we do need. We won't be allowed in any stores. How about getting us a bag of ice and a case of water. I'm so tired of drinking warm soda pops."

"All right I'll be back in a few minutes and then check on Rufus. Make sure he is properly fed and watered." Sterling returns with the ice and water. Then checks on Rufus. "All right got ya'll taken care of. I'll be back Wednesday afternoon to check on ya'll. Oh if it rains tomorrow stay in your tents or get on the porch. Do not get wet. See ya'll Wednesday."

Stepping through the door into the den, "I'm ho-------me honey. Something smells good."

Charlene meets him in the living room with a hug and kiss. "Glad you're home baby. I've got spaghetti and meat balls in tomato spaghetti sauce. Texas toast in the oven."

"Sure smells good, making me hungry."

"You did go over and check on the two campers and their dog?"

"Sure did and they are all right for now. Burt had enough sense to walk over to his house and get his pickup to get around in. Hey they tried to go to work but Stan wouldn't let em. Ole Daniel had them treed. Wouldn't let them in."

"Well what happened. They should have known they couldn't go to work in that condition."

"Well they wrangled a couple of weeks of vacation. Went by doctor Nichols to find out if he would consider cleaning them. But he was closed with a note on his office door. Said he was gone deep sea fishing for about a week. won't be back until next Wednesday. So maybe he can help them.

"Well I don't know why they didn't go with their scout troops and get cleaned, last Saturday evening. Oh thats right he didn't have time to get them."

"Yep he was getting ready to leave for his fishing trip."

"Oh Sterling, changing the subject to a better one. I have a luncheoun meeting tomorrow. And I also got a phone call from another church music minister wanting me to lead their music in their revival. It is a church in Ocean Springs. I told him I would be glad to lead it. It'll be the first week in September. The church will make accomendations for me."

"Hey, I'm glad to hear that, I'm proud of you, baby."

"*Oh, oh, oh! No, no, no! The toast is burning!* Come on baby, and sit down. I'll try to clean the toast up some. Didn't burn as bad as I thought. Just a little scraping." Sterling walks into the kitchen and sits down at the table. Charlene places a glass of iced sweet tea on the table. Sterling takes a drink. "Oh, Sterling it has ten ice cubes. Gotchya." She set a couple of plates down on the table. "Here ya go baby, hope you enjoy it."

"Thank you, it sure smells good. Lets have the thanks and blessings."
A-men, and a-men. Now lets enjoy this dish. Allright----------"

Sterling, baby, think you might could take a week of vacation and go
with me? It would also be a great vacation for us too. We could get a room
on the beach, and enjoy sun set walks along the water's edge. Or early
mornings out on a beach watching the soft warm glow of the sun as it rises.
Sea gulls floating on a soft morning breeze, siloutted in the brightening
sun. It'll be a five day, well night revival. Oh didn't mean to interrupt."

"Thats okay, you know I was just going to ask you the same thing. I'll
get the request in tomorrow. It'll be a great opportunity. And I'll still have
a couple more days. I'll help in any way possible during the services too.
Now this is good baby. I do appreciate it."

Sterling, what are you going to do about Burt and Milt? It is going to
be really hard for them another week."

"Well can't help that, unless I could find another vet somewhere,
who might take a smell at them. I just hope it don't rain much tomorrow.
They get wet it'll be worse than anticipated. Well they are able to provide
for themselves. They walked over to Burt's house and got his dodge
powerwagen. So they aren't stranded, and they can get food and drinks.
just have to go through the dirve ins. If they need anything from the
store I'll go and get it for em. Plus that neighbor hood looks similar to a
futureristic sicfy. No one but them is there. Kinda expected to see them
come out blonde and blue eyed with leather strips weilding double barreled
shotguns."

"Ha, ha Sterling you're so funny. When I get through my luncheon
meeting tomorrow, I'll swing by and check on them too. If they can make
it another week Doctor Nichols probably would be the only one who could
get them clean. Bet they won't do that again. Baby I feel a head ache trying
to come on. I'm really not feeling to well, I'm going to lay down."

"Hey if it's allright I'll come on to. I'll lay, well set up and read. I'm a
bit tired too."

"Then how about lets put a movie in and watch it. Just keep the
volume down."

Tuesday afternoon Sterling arrives home from work, Charlene meets
him at the door with a smile and kiss. "Sterling, Sterling, Sterling. When

I got out of the meeting it was rainning and I went over to see about the outdoor campers. Well they were drowned rats and smelled worse."

"What were they doing? playing in the rain? I told them not to get wet."

"Well baby, they are one hot mess. And Rufus is dry as a bone. Just about begged to come home with me."

"Well they are going to have to wait until next Wednesday. I'll take another vacation day and be sure they are at his office, when he opens. I'll go over and check on them tomorrow afternoon."

Wednesday Sterling punches out of work, and drives to the happy campers. Getting out of his pickup, a strong undescrible scent waffles in the hot humid air. He has to put a hand over his face to block the oder a minute. "Burt, Milt, didn't I tell ya'll not to get wet?" While they stepped down the stepts from the porch.

Burt said, "when we got up yesterday morning it was already raining lightly. You know we do have body functions that does require us to go out. I told Milt that maybe it'll rain really hard and could scrub this stuff off. I had a stranger to go into the dollar store and get us a bottle of body wash. He was a bit smart, about it too, said we needed more than a bottle." We waited until it really started rainning and pulled our shirts and pants off went to the back yard and started lathering and scrubbing. But it only made the situation worse. All we got was wet and cold. I could end up with the flu, by the time this is over."

Milt said, "yea, yes, I thought too that we might get lucky and scrub it off. Plus we'll be out of work more should we get sick. And I miss Ann, Junior, and Joni so bad."

"Me, me, me too, I want Janie Carol back here and have a wonderful night in our bed, so bad.

Waving his hands in front of his face Sterling said, "Well we'll just have to wait until next Wednesday. Um Charlene is trying to get in touch with doctor Nichols to be sure he'll be back Wednesday. But so far no luck. But any way I'm taking off next Wednesday, to help ya'll. I'm quite sure he'll be back as he said. We'll be there before he opens. *Whew!* I'll check on you two during the weekend. Good bye."

Burt said, "yea, bye Sterling." Sterling backs out waving at them.

"See ya'll sometime Saturday." He drives into the drive at home. Entering their home, Charlene meets him with a hug and kiss.

"How are the two campers?"

"They are allright. Not starving, done dried out but stinking worse than ever now. It is a wonder the City mayor don't have them picked up, and carried off."

"Now Sterling we can't let that happen. What will they do? They can't survive out in the wilderness."

"Baby I'm not going to let that happen. If I have to go over and guard them. Hey how have you been doing today?"

I'm doing good, going to get a shower and get ready to go to prayer meeting. I made a tuna fish salad for dinner. I'll put it on a leaf of lettuce or make a sandwich for you honey."

"That sounds good, I can make a sandwich or two. Then I'll get cleaned up and be ready to go with you. I'll give a report on our two campers and still ask to have them on the prayer list.

CHAPTER 10

CLEAN UP

Reverend Stockon stands in the pulpit opening the meeting with a prayer. After the A-men, he looks out over the membership in attendance. "Welcome to prayer meeting. Hope every one is having a good week so far. Does anyone here have a praise testimony, they would love to share?" After a couple of people share an experience, Reverend stockon arrives back at the pulpit. "Now Brother Don, will you come and lead us in a couple of hymns?"

The short stocky middle aged short haired man replies. "Yes I woud love too." The assistance pianist moves quickly to the piano, taking his place and starts playing a light, lively tune. After a couple of hymns, Reverend stockon stepts back to the pulpit. "okay now, does anyone have any prayer requests. A few is shared for the sick and hospitialized, and a couple of minor surgeries coming up for people in the community. As a quiteness envelopes the chapel, Reverend Stockon asked. "Sterling how are the Crystal Springs, neighbor hood campers doing?"

Sterling stands and ask for permission to come down front and shares a report on the two campers. "So next Wednesday July six, I am going to help them with their cleanup at doctor Lance Nichols office. He'll be back in and as soon as he opens we'll be waiting. So ya'll please be in prayer that he can get them clean, and rosy again." At the end of the service, Reverend stockon said. "And remember, at Hopewell Baptist Church. Enter to worship and depart to serve."

After good bye hand shakes, Charlene finds Sterling. "Hi baby, I'm ready to go home. Got a bit of a head ache, and not feeling very good."

"Yes, I'm ready to go too. See you at home."

Entering the door, Charlene turns to Sterling hugging and kissing him. "Honey I'm going to bed. I really don't feel good. Hey we did have a great choir practice. We have a great patriotic song for the special message in music for Sunday. It is featuring three solos, and Mrs. Rose is singing one. I'm singing one and Don said he would sing the other. I'm going to take one of my pain tablets and get some releif. I love you my man."

"Hope you'll get to feeling better when you get some relief. I'm coming on to bed too. Got to get up early and go to work. "I love you to, my dear."

Sterling setting at the table in his worship and devotion time, before going to work. He gets up and pours one more cup of coffee, before getting primped up for the day. Charlene walks into the kitchen, "good morning my love."

"Good morning. You must be feeling better?"

"Yes I feel really good and rested now. Those pain pills doctor Bellows prescribed for me really does the job. By the time we laid down last night I could feel the head ache easing off. I'll be at the church office most of today. I would have a cup of coffee with you, but I want to get a little more sleep. Could be a long day as I've got some counseling to do.

"Well when I get off from work I'm going by to check on the campers, and then I'll be on home."

"Okay, I've got to go to the bathroom and then back to bed for a while. Have a great day, and I love you my man."

About to ease out of the house, Sterling peeks in on Charlene, and turns to leave. "Sterling, I'm not asleep yet come on back in here. I need that hug before you go."

Sterling leans down to give her a hug and kiss. Hey I love you baby. I've got to be headed up the highway."

"I love you too, be careful now."

Monday morning July fourth, Sterling arrives on a sandbar, of bayou Pierrie creek on the hunting club lease. Staring into the early dawn light in the east a light blue and pink sunlit sky and white, blue clouds dots the sunrise. He sets his box of jigs on a log at the water's edge. With a yellow jig tied on the end of his line, he encounters the cool, well cold shallow flowing water, swirling around his ankles as he slowly makes his way out to a couple of logs that lay about waist deep, in the creek. Finally becoming acclimated to the cold water he drops the jig down beside a log and waits a coulpe of minutes for the jig to Settle on the bottom. Hoping a yearling bass would grab it on it's fall. But nothing hits. He slowly raises the jig to the surface and allows it to drop again. Then working it a little faster a bass grabs it hard and swims fast into the faster current, when the hook is set. Putting the two pounder on the stringer, he wades back out to the log. Instantly another one, attempts a hit and run, then succombs to the set hook. *'wow!'* He thinks to himself I'm going to have a mess of fish quickly. If I can get six or eight more I'm heading home and have a fish fry. Charlene loves this kind of fish. They'll go good with a couple of chicken breasts. Wading out to another log, see if there is any fish under this one. A couple of times around the log he brings the jig back toward deeper water when the pole bends with a fight. He finally brings this one to him. He reaches down into the water grabbing the fish in it's mouth and lifts it up. looking at the elogated head with green scales gleaming in the bright sunlight. *'This one will go about three, maybe four pounds. fillet him.'*

After a few more wrestling matches, he puts the tenth fish on the stringer. Looking at his watch, nine o'clock. *'I have enough for a good cooking. Stop at the camp and clean these fish put'em on ice and go home.'* Arriving at his pickup, laying the stringer of fish in the bed, he then reaches into his ice chest and pulls out a coke. Then he gets his pole tied down and drives out to the camp, and does the cleaning chores. That done and cleaning his knife blade he grabs another coke and drives home.

Entering the house Charlene is just getting coffee made. As he saunters to the scent of coffee, Charlene said. "Good morning honey. What ya got there?"

"Hey baby, I had a great morning in the creek. Got these ten bass. Could've caught more, but this is enough for us. I'm going to fry'em later."

"They must a been biting today. How about lets go back out there Saturday morning. I bet I can catch more than you."

"I'll take you up on that. Hey got enough coffee made to share a cup or two?

Sure do honey. Here hand me that bag of fish. Set down and I'll bring you a cup. With three teaspoons of sugar in it. Would you like a egg or two and some bacon?"

"Not really, just this coffee. I'm going to the living room and catch a western show. Gun Smoke, The Cartwrights or something. Nap between the programs and then get the out door cookers warmed up and fry those fish with a few chicken breasts and thighs."

"Hey, baby I'll make the slaw and peel a few potatoes."

After a episode of Gunsmoke and Bonanza, he gets up walks into the kitchen opening the refridgerator and pours himself a glass of tea. "Charlene, baby, I'm headed out to the back yard and get the cooker started."

"Okay honey I'll get the fish breaded and bring them out." Reling, reling, reling. "Hello."

Burt said "Hello Charlee."

"Hi Burt, you and Milt are all right aren't ya'll?"

"Well yes and no, I need to speak with Sterling. Is he anywhere close by?"

"Yes, he is right out back. Been out fishing this morning and now we are going to cook the catch." Charlene walks to the kitchen door looking out. "Sterling it's for you."

Sterling walks briskly to the phone. Charlene said as she handed the receiver to him. "It's Burt, something might be wrong. I hope not."

Sterling speaks into the receiver, "Hello Burt, whats going on?"

"Sterling; Milt and I just can't stand this stuff anymore. Our neighbor hood has finally evacuated, and a couple of city councilmen have visited us wearing gas masks. But we finally got them to leave us alone, because our homes are paid for and it would take a city ordaince and court order to remove us. Plus Milt can't hardly get close enough to Rufus to feed and water him. He has to pour his food over the fence and spray the water from a distance to his pan. I told ole Hambone, and Erick the red, that we were going Wednesday to get cleaned by doctor Nichols. Sterling it is really bad. Especially after we got wet the other day when it rained. I'm sick and tired of camping."

"well, I went fishing this morning and caught a few bass."

"You did! Sterling dog gone it. That after noon out on that creek I fished and fished and didn't get a nibble. What'd you use for bait?"

"I took my cane pole and a couple of jigs, one yellow and the other white. Right at day light I waded out into the creek about waist deep to a couple of logs. And in the next hour or so I had over ten bass. I'm getting ready to fry them and some chicken. I have enough for ya'll if you'd like a plate."

"Yes I would enjoy a plate of fish and chicken, especially bass. Hold on a sec. Milt!"

Milt answers, "yes."

Burt asks him, "Sterling caught a bunch of fish this morning and wants to know if you would like a plate of fish and chicken?"

Milt answers excitedly, "Yes I would."

Burt said, "Sterling we'll be looking for you later. Hey can you bring us a gallon of sweet tea and a couple bags of ice?"

Sterling answers, "Okay, I'll be glad to. As soon as I get a some cooked I'll bring it right on."

Burt said, "Sterling you are a good friend. Even though you tell things that seem so real, and make just about anyone believe it."

"Aw come on Burt, you know that ain't so. I'll be right over when I get some done. I'll see you two later. Good bye."

Later Sterling drives into Milt's drive and steps out. *'Aw, man!' this scent is worse than what I dared to think it could be.'* Walking around the house, to the back yard. He takes note of a ghost town like neighbor hood much like in the old western movies ghost towns. Milt meets him just as he turns by the rear corner of the house.

"Hey Sterling!" Milt exclaims in excitement. Sterling jumps being startled. Nearly throwing the aluminum foiled covered pan of fish, fries and coleslaw up and over his head."

Recovering lightning fast, Serling responded. "Why Milt ole buddy ole pal. I have ya'll a good dinner here. Take it, while I go back to my pickup and get the couple bags of ice and tea." Sterling returns to the back yard with the ice and tea. "Here ya'll go. And Burt I also got you a couple of ice cold Bud's. I sure hope ya'll enjoy it. Hope it is enough. I see you two have this whole neighbor hood to roam in. Kind of similar to being in the wilderness eh?"

Burt said, Oh yea right, We are the only ones here at the moment. But ain't gonna go roaming around these houses. Even here ain't no telling what could be waiting for us. Hey these fish is still hot and crisp. It sure does smell good. Lets eat before this gets cold and soggy."

Sterling said, "Well I'm headed back home. Remember Wednesday morning I'll meet you two at Doctor Nichols office at eight o'clock."

Milt said. "Even if we do get cleaned it'll still be a while before Ann comes home."

Burt said, "It'll probably be a longer time before Jaine decides to come back, if she does. I've got to do some sweet talking, to convince her I am clean and fresh again."

"Well," Sterling said, "When ya'll get clean and fresh you can move in with Charlene and I, until the western style women heads back East. That will allow you two to get back to work. Burt I'll even take you fishing in the creek. Show you how to catch those fish."

Chuckling, Burt said, "After I eat this fish, I don't think I'll want to get within sight of that creek. Once I get cleaned again I just might give up fishing. Just buy a few pounds every now and then from Wilson's or Wal-Mart."

"Ha, haaaa, haaaaaaaa, Burt you know you won't quit fishing. You can stay in the safety of the lakes and ponds nearby. This ain't no reason to just give up."

Burt exclaimed, "Shoot! Who knows I might take up golf with my other buddies and customer reps, I deal with each day. Bet they'll be glad to see me back in the sales deprtment." Pooosha, Burt pops the can of beer open. "Sterling this is great. This Bud is good with these yearling bass. I sure do appreciate you thinking of us today."

Milt said, "Yea, thank you Sterling and give Charlene my regards, and be sure to thank her for us too."

"Sterling said. "Well I'm heading back home. I'll see you to at doctor Nichols Wednesday morning at eight. So see ya'll there. so long."

"Good bye Sterling," Milt said, We'll be there."

Milt returns to the picnic table sitting down getting his portion of the fish dinner. "Burt said. "Milt, you know ole Silver is a great guy. He hasn't really left us alone over here."

"Yea, he has been good to us. And even going to let us come into his home until we can get ours open again. You know I really miss Ann, Milt and Joni Ann. I just hope she'll come back when I call her in a couple of days. Me and Junior is going to take up something else.

"I know that Milt." "I'm going to spend more clean and quality time with Jan, Beth and June. Don't think I'll let them get into the girl scouts. Charlene might take them out on a feild trip or something. No telling what Sterling might have her up too. Knowing her, she'd do it too."

"And I would'nt put it past her either. Man this is good. Wonder how he learned to cook like this."

Arriving back home Charlene meets him with a hug and kiss. "Honey, I'm glad you are making sure those campers are all right. Were they excited to get the fish dinner?"

"Sure was. Probably the first home cooked meal they've had in over a week. They are all right, except the neighbor hood is desolate. Looks like some in an end of time mystery novel."

"Well I wonder what mystery caused that?"

"I was looking at any moment for some muscular blue eyed blond dude wearing chains and leather garments, that seems to be a couple of sizes too small, toting a sawed off double barrel shotgun. He probably shot the critter he was wearing with it, and tanned it's hide. One could expect him to jump out any moment."

With hands on her hips, "I wonder why. Baby, I've got to lay down a while I have a bad headache, thats making me sick."

"I'll slip into the living room and let you rest. If you need anything let me know. I'm going to see if the Atlanta braves are playing."

Hugging her she said. "I'll be okay when this headache eases. It's bad enough to take a pain pill, and it has me a little sleepy and dizzy. When I get up later, we'll watch a movie." Toward the end of the game charlene get up and wonders into the living room. "Hi Sterling want a bowl of popcorn to go with the movie?"

"Sure would, ain't much of a movie without cokes and popcorn." Getting the movie rolling, they snuggle up on the couch. When the movie ends, Sterling stands up. "Well I need to be getting in the bed. Got to get early and go back to work."

"I'm coming to bed with you, while this headache is eased. I'm getting sleepy again. I'll be in the office most of tomorrow to. Working on the song worship for Sunday. Going back to doctor Bellows Wednesday morning. I'm going to watch the news and weather. I'll keep the volume on the lower side so it won't disturb ya."

"Hey you ain't bothering me, by laying in the bed watching the television."

Getting settled in the bed Charlene reaches over and kisses him, "I love you my man."

"I sure do love you too pretty lady."

Tuesday morning, eleven o'clock the bell rings for the thirty minute lunch break. He walks out to his pickup, spotting Charlene as she turns into a space close to his. He picks up his pace to her. She emergs from the Surburban, with a sonic bag of two cheeseburgers and fries. "Hi honey, I was able to get away from the church office for a while and had you on my mind. Thought we would have lunch together."

"Hey baby," giving her a hug and kiss, "glad you was able to do this. I appreciate it."

Making a quick picnic table on the tail gate of his pickup. "Baby how's your day going?"

"Ahh about as usual. I'll finish a big job I am woking on later. Then before I get off I'll set up for the job I'll be working on tomorrow. It'll be a little easy this afternoon."

"Don't let'em work you more than you're getting paid. I've got to be headed back to the office now." Kissing him good bye. "As always and forever I love you my man."

"I love you too. And again thank you for bringing lunch. I'll go by and check on Milt and Burt when I get off work. I have a vacation day lined up for tomorrow. Just hope doctor Nichols can get them clean. I'll see you later." He turns to go back into the factory as she leaves out. waving at him. He waves back with a smile, blowing her a kiss.

Sterling turns into the drive, spotting Milt and Burt setting on the steps of the porch. Sterling walks to them. "Hey professional campers. Guess what."

Milt said, "professional campers, heck we ain't no campers. We're only out here because this is the only place we can be. You hear any thing from doctor Nichols?"

"Yep, he finally called me just a couple of hours ago. He said for ya'll to be at his office at seven, tomorrow morning."

Burt said, "We'll certianly be there. Even a few minutes early, waiting on him. So we were just waiting for you to come by. So now I'm a bit releived, that he is going to try and help us. Milt you wanna lets go and get a burger and fries for dinner after while. In fact I sure could use another cold bud. See if we can catch someone who will go in and get a six pack."

"Burt I'll go down to the store and get you a six pack. Milt any soft drinks you'd like?"

"Yes get me a couple of cokes. I just don't like the taste of beer."

Burt reaching into his back pocket for his wallet. "Here Sterling take this and get our drinks."

"Ummmm, no Burt, I'll get them for ya'll. And look Burt you don't need to drink much now. Y'all can't miss this doctor's appointment. It's your only shot. Be back in a minute." Sterling returns with the six pack and a couple of cokes. "Okay here ya'll go. I may come over here around six tomorrow morning. Be sure ya'll are ready. So I'll see ya'll round six. Good bye."

Sterling arrives home at the same time Charlene drives into the drive. They meet in the yard, with a hug and kiss. "The campers still okay?"

"Yep, and they can't wait till tomorrow morning. I told them that I would be back a little early to be sure they are up and ready. In which I'm sure they will be. hahahaaaaahaaaa, they are so tired of camping."

"And they are in a different wilderness too. Sterling I've got a doctor appointment in the morning too. Doctor Bellows called me right after lunch and said he wanted to see me. I have the appoinment at eight thirty. When I get through I'll come over to doctor Nichols to find out about Milt and Burt's cleaning is going. Hey I'm more tired than usual and I know you are tired too. Since we don't have to get up real early tomorrow morning how about lets ride down to Brookhaven and have dinner at Cracker Barrel."

"Yes that'll be great. I'm going in to change clothes and we'll head out."

"I'll make a quick change and freshen up too."

Buzzzzzzzzzz, buzzzzzzzzzz, buzzzzzzzzz, Sterling wakes up and reaches over turning the snooze on. It is already four thirty. Lay back down a few more minutes. Ten minutes later the buzzing stings him in his head as he raises up. Well get on up and get a pot of coffee made and then I'll wake nappy head up. Coffee made he pours himself a cup and sets down at the table, opening his Bible to the book being read and studied. After reading a couple of chapters he pours himself another. Then walks to the bed room, easing over to Charlene. "All right sleeping bueaty I have coffee made if you'd like a cup."

"What time is it baby?"

"It'sabout five fifteen. Getting ready to go over to get Milt and Burt up."

"Just reset the clock for around six forty five. I'll check on ya'll when I get out of doctor Bellows office."

"All right. I'll reset the cofee pot for you, then I'll ease on out."

"Sterling I sure hope he can get those two completly clean. Because Janie called last night after you went to sleep. She was asking about her Burt. I told her that Doctor Nichols was going to attempt a cleaning on those two. And she asked me if I'd let Burt call her tonight should they get cleaned. And we were going to let them stay with us until she and Ann could get home. So tell both of them that the wives does miss them after all."

Around ten minutes till seven Milt and Burt follows Sterling into the vet's parking lot. As they are getting out of the dodge power wagen doctor Lance Nichols, a middle age, tall slender dressed in tan kakis with a blue dress shirt. Walking to the door unlocking it, then looking at Milt and Burt. "Wow, that stuff hasn't lost a bit of power yet." Looking at Sterling. What is that concoction you had them to put on. Had a time with those younguns. Hope I can do ya'll some good. Might take two or three treatments over the next couple of weks. But we'll see what we can do today and go from there."

Burt said, "Bu-bu-bbbbut, we have to be clean today so we can get back to work Monday. All we have is till Monday."

Milt butted in. "Yea doc Nochols, we don't have any more time to be off. Plus I'm ready to get back into my home with my wife and kids. I've had enough camping to last a half dozen life times."

"*Whew! That smell is worse than those younguns.* Well ya'll come on in and lets get started before my regulars come in. Some of them may want to eat ya'll, plus others probably will want to roll on ya." Entering his office.

"See that room to the right in the back? Go in there and wait a minute. My wife and secretary will be here in just a minute."

"Sterling I'm going on back there and get started. They are going to have to soak in a strong dog shampoo in as hot a water as they can stand. Then I have some cleaner that I clean pets and people who have been sprayed by skunks. It works good on that but this all I can is try."

"okay," Sterling replied, "When Brenda comes in I'll let you know." About ten minutes pass when the door creaks open as Brenda enters swaying her dress.

"Oh hi Sterling, I can smell Milt and Burt have already arrived."

"Sterling greets, "good morning," while noticing her perfectly spread makeup and lipstick, taking in her long tall form in a brown dress matching her brown eyes, long brown hair. 'what does a woman like this want with Lance Nichols. Oh well'

"Sterling! Quit sizing me up! I ain't gonna marry you."

"I wouldn't size you up. Just admiring your beauty."

"Ain't you a romantic! Oh and look at what you did to the future of this city and county, and those two soon to be history. Boy, Lance has got to hurry up and get them clean. That sent is more than awful."

Lance walks back to the office handing Brenda, Milt and Burt's credit cards. "Brenda, run these cards for two hundred dollars each. Thats what it will cost to get them clean. Sterling then they want you to go and buy them a couple of changing of clean clothes. Here is their sizes in jeans and shirts. Might as well get them at least five sets apeice. Their clothes are gone. I put them out."

Brenda hands Sterling the cards. "Here ya go Sterling go get'em a few sets of jeans and shirts. Don't come back for a while." As Sterling opens the door Charlene walks in. Brenda looking at Sterling to see what he has to say. She turns her head to the side hands on her hips with eyes rolled up mimmichs him. "Oh hi Baby. Ooooooweeeee, ain't you a doll today." Then she throws her head back ahhhhhhh. Then says to herself. 'Oh such a smoothie.'

"Thank you my dearest man. Our campers got started yet?"

"Brenda chimes in. "Good morning Charlene. Lance has them back there in a couple of tubs soaking. They'll have to soak at least and hour.

Then he'll change the water and start scrubbing them. Ought to put Sterling back there scrubbing them."

Sterling said 'I'm headed out to get Milt and Burt a few sets of clothes. Jeans, tee shirts, socks and a couple pair of shoes."

"Well baby," Charlene said, better let me do that. I'll go when I get out of doc Bellows. See ya'll after while. I love you my man. Then kisses him and leaves."

"I love you too, pretty lady," as she closes the door behind him."

Brenda looking at him hahahahahahahah, still stuck with you I see. Aw Sterling go on over there and sit down."

Sterling said, "Since it is going to be a while, I'm going over to McDonalds and eat breakfast. Want me to bring you something back?"

"Yes, if you don't mind, Bring me and Lance a sausage and bisquit with egg and cheese meal back. With coffees."

"Sure will I'll just go over there and get them and come on back. Be back in a few minutes."

"Here Sterling, I've got to get you the money for the breakfast."

"Brenda, don't worry about that I'll get it."

Walking back in with the three breakfasts. Brenda says, "Sterling just put the bag here. I'll go get Lance and see if he can come out and eat. We don't have any patients until another hour or so." She walks to the back knocking on a door.

"Lance said, "Yes, what is it?"

"Brenda said, "Lance honey, Sterling went and got us breakfast. Would you like to take a few minutes and eat?"

"Sure would. I'll be on out when I get my hands washed." He enters into the office area. "Sure smells great in here. I'm hungry. Lets eat."

Doctor Nichols said as he finished. "Thank you Sterling. I'm ready to start scrubbing now. Should ya'll hear any whinning and hollering, just go outside for a while. Right before the first patient comes in doctor Nichols brings them out wrapped in animal robes and skin red from the scrubbing. Leading them to his private office, and closes the door. Their hair portions fluffed and parts resembling stickers in a clump of grass.

Sterling asks, "ya'll feel better now?"

Stepping into the private office, for privacy, Milt looks back at Sterling. "Yes Sterling, other than being almost raw, the scent isn't as bad a it was. Hope this don't take much longer."

After seeing his first two patients, he walks to the office knocks on the door. "Okay you two come on. See if we can get this done before any more patients arrive. Burt said all most crying. "I got to go through this scrubbing again? I've been partially scalped. Now I'm being skint."

Milt said, "and I'm not. Anythingto get this stinking stuff off."

Doctor Nichols said, "all right this is the only way I know of to get ya'll clean again. One more round and it should be done. A little bit of what ever that is, is still adhered to your skin. I'v got some good dog skin lotion for ya'll when we get through. It'll cool the redness.

A couple of hours later Charlene enters the office with a big smile. "Hi, I'm b--a--c--k. "that just lightens the office up."

Brenda getting up and walking out to help Charlene with the bags of clothes. "Here Charlene let me help you with that. Ole western over there isn't."

"Oh Brenda, I just wanted to show you what I got for them. Hadn't had so much fun shopping in a long time."

"Was it because you didn't have Sterling following you around."

Pulling out a couple of Roper jeans. "I found these on special today. Ropers, wow make them western hounds again."

Doctor Nichols enters back into the office. "Well I finally have them clean. We'll wait about a half hour to let the lotion soothe them and be sure they are clean and fresh."

Charlene said, "oh I got them some colonge to." Looking at Sterling. "And no it's not your repellant."

Doctor Nichols said, "Sterling I really don't know what you had them put on but it wasn't going to come off. That is some bad stuff." Then he walks back into the treatment rooms. "Okay Milt and Burt, let me smell ya'll to be sure no futher scrubbing is necessary. All right go on out into my office and get dressed."

As they shuffle into the private office a sly grin comes across Sterling. "Hey, don't you two smell sweet now."

Brenda and Charlene fires a flurry of looks at Sterling. A few minutes later they emerge clean and rosy. Burt said. "Charlene thank you for getting us the colonge so we can smell good again. Better than what Sterling has."

Doctor Lance sniffs over them one more time. "Okay I do think we've got this stuff off you. Ya'll are free to go now. And don't be putting any unknown stuff on ya. Especially if Sterling made it."

Exiting the building Brenda said, "Charlene, Sterling it was good visiting ya'll. Come back sometime."

"Charlene, I'll let them ride with me home. Starting to climb into the bed of the pickup, Sterling commanded, "Ya'll get up here with me."

Charlene said, "Ya'll can stay with us until your high sheriff women gets back. I've stayed in touch with them. And yes they are ready to come back to the hosendas. Tonight you can call them."

Starting the Chevy S-10 pickup, "you two western heros hungry?"

Burt said, "Sure are, where ya'll want to eat at."

Sterling answered, "Well I thought we'd get a burger and fries, for lunch and then for dinner this afternoon Charlene will get a couple of large pizzas and a movie."

Milt looking at Sterling, "yes that sounds great, I'll buy lunch."

Sterling said, "Nope, nope, nope Charlene and I will take care of this. Lets go get a bite to eat and then go home for a while."

Burt said, "sounds good to me. Be good once again to relax in a air conditioned home." Driving into McDonalds in Hazlehurst. Rubbing his hair, Burt said, "don't know what they are going to think about our hair doos."

Entering the restaurant, three young boys begin laughing at their hair, and wisphering to each other."

Sterling walks over to them in a slow gait with hands on his belt buckle, stethson pulled low. "And what are ya'll laughing at? Attracting attention from other people eating lunch. Believe me I wouldn't be staring at them too much."

"Oh yea, mister, what happened to them, a house cat got'em?" hahahahaaaaaaaaahhhhhhaa.

Sterling bends down over them putting his hands on the table. One of them starts to hit his hand with the stock of a pocket knife. "Hey son I wouldn't do that. See those two men ya'll are making fun of. Don't judge them by their cover. We just got back from a African photo safri. Hunting, photographing real wild and free amimals in the African bush. On our own, no outfitter, guide or professional hunter. One evening we were crawling through some really sticky thick thickets looking for our prey. Gonna get a close up photo of that python we saw slither into the thicket. As we slowly stalked farther into the thicket we encounterd a marsh" Sterling jumps quickly looking to the side. Causing them to jump. Trying to contain his laughter. When right upon us a three hundred pound leapord, cold yellow eyes and sharp claws protuding in his pounce on us. Well that tall dude grabbed him as his hair was flying off. He lifted him up and body slammed him to the ground. I thought I heard the cats ribs crushing as he jumped up wagging that long tail and side hopped out of there. And that short dumpy one? Well I wouldn't exactly call him dumpy to his face. Because the next day we continued our search for that giant annaconda. The marsh was getting a bit deeper, when a eruption busted out of the water. Water, mud, weeds were flying all around. A six or seven hundred pound fifteen or so foot long crockadile, was up and violently shaking him from side to side. He happened to swim head first into the crock's mouth. Well he grabbed that crock around his throat choking the em down, had a death grip. All I could see was arms and hands around that croc's throat, and legs protruding out of the jaws. Man that crock was shaking him around. The tall one instantly had that crock by the hind legs pulling him. Then the short one began hitting that crock in his throat with his bare fist. The blows sounded like hundred mile per hour fast balls slamming into a catcher's mit. Tat giant finally turned him loose. Finally they got him under control and drug em up on a log, so he would'nt drown. Now you wanna go up there and call him dumpy? I'd put that little toy knife back in my pocket. So when he was able to stand up and get a breath, his hair was all that was messed up. Not one scratch on'em."

The young brown haired freckled faced youth slowly slipped the knife back into his pocket. "Sir, are they friendly?"

"Yep, the best friends you'd want. After that ordeal they don't take too kindly to people laughing at their hair. The other two agast and speechless got up, started walking to the door.

"Hey ya'll don't have to leave."

"turning around, one of them said. "Well we need to be going anyway, got other places to go." Milt and Burt got their trays of food, turning around looking at the three youths. Their eyes widened in fright, exiting the door quickly." Milt said as he set down watching the small Chevy Colorado pickup drive out the drive and speed down the highway. "Those boys left in a hurry, like they seen a ghost."

Burt said while taking a bite out of his quarter pounder. "It sure feels great to sit in a restaurant and eat again. Man it is good." Looking around noticing the attention they were getting. "Why are all these people staring at us?"

Milt looks up from his burger looking back at a couple watching them, and fires a hard stare back. Instantly the man and woman, turns back to their dinner as if they were not staring at the two men.

Finishing lunch Sterling said, "Ya'll ready to head on to the hosenda?"

"Yes," Milt said, and stretch out again and get comfortable."

Entering the house, Charlene asks, "ya'll still clean?" Approaching Sterling and kissing him. "In a couple of hours I'll go and get the pizzas and a movie. What would ya'll like to watch?"

Burt answers, "get a detective drama, or love story. Just don't bring home anything about camping."

"Ok that reminds me of a movie I've been thinking about renting, it'll be right down your alley. Jacks Back. I'll get that one. Would ya'll like anything to drink or eat? Well ya'll just make yourselves at home. If you want something just go and get it."

Sterling sets down in is recliner, next to Charlene in hers. Burt and Milt sets on each end of the sofa and lets it down to a recliner. Anything special on television ya'll would want to watch?"

Burt said, "um not really I don't know whats on this time of day. I'm gonna just relax and nap for a while."

Milt replied, "I am too." A few minutes pass and they are snoring lightly. Charlene said. "Look Sterling those two are so worn out and tired after their ordeal. Don't do that to em anymore."

"Well baby, how'd your doc's appointment go?"

"Oh, we haven't had time to discuss it have we. Both of us been busy with those two. Doctor Bellows thinks it could be migraines. I'll talk with him more on the fifteenth when both of us goes back. I'm going to slip on out and get the pizzas and the movie.

Milt and Burt wakes up just before Charlene returns. "Ya'll been sleeping mighty hard. Like ye was tired or something."

Burt said, "yea, couldn't help but to sleep. Ain't been this comfortable in a while. Bet I'll sleep good tonight too."

Charlene enters back in, "Hi ya'll, hungry? Hope so."

Milt said getting up, "here Charlee, let me help with that."

"I've got it Milt." She walks into the kitchen placing the pizzas on the table. and sets a few paper plates beside them. "Okay, ya'll come on and make your plates while I get the movie started."

Sterling sets out the tv trays as they return.

After the movie ends, Charlene said, "now that was a really good movie. Well it is seven o'clock, ya ladies ought to be back in by now. Burt lets call and see if Jan is back at her parent's. Hello oh yes Jan I thought your mother had answered. I have someone here who you might like to speak with. Here Burt."

Burt answers, "Hi Jan, my honey bunch, sugar pie, sweet bread, I really have missed you and the kids."

"Aw Burt honey, you just don't know how much I've missed hearing those words. I heard earlier today ya'll got cleaned. Really clean?"

"Yes, doc, Nichols had to scrub us twice after soaking in some hot water solution for over an hour. And still that scent did'nt want to come off. I was all but skint, but now that it's over I feel really good now."

"I'm glad you do, and honey I'll be home in the next couple of days. Can't wait to be back with you. And look don't let that ole skunk and bear man spray and pee on you."

"Oh I won't fall for that again, don't have any desires to go out to the creek anymore. Especially that area. Well Sterling and Charlene is getting ready for bed now and I need to get off. Um Milt wants to call Ann. Hey I sure do love you. And if you get a chance call me tomorrow here. Charlene and Sterling has opened their home to us. He said he would go and take those tents down and take em to the dump."

Okay Burt, if I can I will. I'm helping old friends out here run their business. If not I'll let you know when I'll come home. Can't wait to see you sugar bear. I love you."

"Okay sweet bread I love you too. Good night."

Milt walks out of the bathroom, when the phone rings. Charlene answers, "hello. Oh hi Ann yes he is right here." Hands Milt the phone.

"Hello sweetie pie. Honey I'm clean."

"I certainly hope so. I've really missed you. I can get my return flight tomorrow morning. When we get home we'll be right over there and pick you up. Be sure you thank Charlene for allowing you to stay with them. Don't let that skunk spray you. I'll widen that stripe down his back."

"Ann darling, it really is good to hear your voice. And you're not mad at me anymore."

"Milt I wasn't as angry as you thought I was. But angry enough to get away from that scent.

Hey Milt junior has been asking about you. Yep grandpa had a good laugh at what he told him about the camp out. Well I'm getting ready to go down for the night. Get a good night's sleep for the flight back. See you sometime tomorrow afternoon. I love you."

"Yep Sterling and Charlene is going to bed. He has got to get up and go back to work tomorrow. And I love you too. Goodnight."

CHAPTER 11

CLEAN REUNION

Sterling said, "Milt and Burt, I'm going to just slip out tomorrow morning. I'll try not to disturb ya'll. Ya'll can set up and watch what ever you want. Ya'll know where every thing is. Just help yourselves. Good night."

Coffee brewing at three thirty in the morning, Sterling pours himself a cup and stirs in a couple of teaspoons of sugar in it and saunters to the table. Sitting down while taking a sip, Burt staggers in. "Good morning Burt, idin't mean to wake you."

"Good morning Sterling, I just woke up and had to go to the bathroom. Coffeee sure smells good."

"Hey there are the cups, and the sugar and cream bowl is right there beside the coffee pot. Just help yourself."

"Okay think I will. "Setting down at the table he takes a sip. "Ah, sure is good Sterling."

"Burt what are you and Milt planning today?"

"Probably nothing much. If it is still all right with you and Charlene we'll probably lazy around here today."

"Sure thats okay with us. Burt reckon you could take your pickup and get it cleaned inside and out. Don't want that scent to get back on ya."

"I'll do that. Was thinking about it, especially before Janie gets home. And Milt probably will be gone home before either one of you two gets back home."

"You don't know exalty, when Janie will come back?"

"Hopefully over the weekend or early part of next week."

"Well if she don't come back by Saturday, wanna go fishing with me? We'll go down on the creek and I'll give you some pointers on how to catch those bass."

"We----ll, I don't know. Maybe, if I don't have to put that repellant on, and we'd be quite safe."

"Na, you won't, and we'll have some fun catching us a mess of fish. Come back and have a fish fry Saturday afternoon."

"Okay we'll do that, get up early Saturday and head out to the creek. I'm going to get one more cup of coffee and then finish getting ready for work and slip on outta here."

Taking his cup to the sink and washing it, "Sterling that was a great cup of coffee. I'm going back to lay down for a while. Have a good day and don't work too hard. After Charlene leaves, we'll go get my pickup cleaned."

"I don't think Charlene is going to have a long day today. Mostly work on the song service for Sunday morning and Sunday night. I'll see you this afternoon. Charlene is going to cook all of us a good home cooked meal. She knows Ann will be tired from jet lag probably when she arrives here. So ya'll have a good day. I'm outta here and headed up the road. Good bye."

Eleven o'clock lunch break Sterling walks out to his pickup as usual. The distance walks is a little exercise. He spots Charlene at the gate waiting for him, stepping his pace up toward her.

"Hi Sterling baby, I was really thinking of you today. You've been real heavy on my mind. I just want to be near you. I'm concerned about something. Voices from the past is calling. I mean really calling. But I just hope I can nip them in the bud quickly. But anyway I just thought I would bring a burger and fries to you."

Sterling opens the gate or her to come in. They embrace and kiss. Then gets in Sterling's pickup. They set there unwrapping their Sonic cheese burgers and begins to eat. "Sterling Sunday is going to be a special Sunday. That is my anniversary day back around twenty five years ago when I was nearly killed in that drug bust as an under cover agent. I had the whole gang together until, ole Loco poco wanted to try something special with me. When he bent down to kiss me in front of the gang. These people were so evil that they were going to start a drug and alchol party where I was going to be the entaintment. They were going to force me to get up on their make shift stage and perform a strip tease, then each one was going to have their turn with me. I nailed him in the face with a compact steel bar. Raked it right across his nose and blood started spurting. That act exposed my wire tap and I called for the attack. Well as Poco was rolling on the floor in his pool of blood another member drew his short .38 Smith. I was still close enough to break his wrist with my bar and the impact sounded as if it took his wrist off the hand.

I was trying to get to my .357 mag, I had stashed in the inside of my garter belt, hoping it would support the weight, when the banging on the doors began as the dea agents were busting in. The door flew open and the commander yelled, "Get outta here, we'll finish this" as gun shots beging popping off. I made it to the street where I collasped in front of the back up team as they were coming for me."

Sterling, I was laying there bleeding. Right here in my right shoulder from behind and low, the bullet expanded as it exited tearing out flesh from my chest. It felt as if I was on fire. From there I don't remember much until I was recovering in the hospital in Atlanta. Sterling Baby I can tell you that there is life after death. Leaving this earth is not final. I died twice, I was out of my body and going into the darkest of places. No light at all. A darkness I don't ever want to experience again. Then I returned to my body. The second time just before we got to the hospital my heart stopped again. Something big and strong had me. And there was no strength to get away from him. As he drug me upwards, I knew this creature hated me with all that was in him. I thought this time I wouldn't come back. Farther and farther away we went. I was pounding on him as hard as I could but he never felt any of my blows. Ya, aaaaaa, yaa, yaaaaa, haaaa, aaaaa. Then I started crying out to the God that my dad always preached about every Sunday. I must've called out with all I had in me to my dad's God. Because my dad heard about it on the news as it happened he began praying for my safety. Then Sterling the most powerful being in ths episode entered the scene and just approached this monster and took me away from him. He escourted me back to my locaton and just before allowing me to go back, he told me to use your singing and other gifts for my glory from now own. You have one more chance for salvation from this. I really want you in my service. Go and do. I promised him right there I would, and asked him if I was saved now or not. He said yes now get baptised. And live for me.

Now I'm informed that those people are to be released or have already been released. I just found that out this morning. Sterling they are coming after me. Knowing them they'll attack you to draw me out. Please baby don't try to be my hero and take them on yourself. I know you want to protect me. But I have a plan, Sterling darling, these are some really bad evil men, that you know nothing about. Please stay aware of your surroundings. I really do love you my man. And be safe in there working. Please don't say anything about this yet. As nothing has actually transpired other than this notification. I'm going shopping for dinner tonight. How about my great meatloaf, mashed potatoes, and fresh corn on the cobb, and of course bisquits."

"Ah yea that'll be good. Hey Burt and I are going fishing tomorrow morning."

Charlene gives that look at Sterling, I dare you do anything else to him. Good bye baby, I love you my man."

"I love you too pretty lady."

During dinner Burt said, while wiping his mouth and hands with the napkin, "Charlee that was really good. I really enjoyed that. Hey did Sterling tell you we were going fishing tomorrow morning?"

Charlene getting up taking Burt's dishes, like another helping? Or ready for dessert?"

"Whats for dessert?"

"Home made apple pie, been cooled in the kitchen window. With or without vanilla ice cream on top of it."

"I'll have a slice of pie with ice cream"

"Milt, Ann how about ya'll?"

Pushing her chair out, Ann said. "Charlene let me help with the dessert. Okay. You've done plenty for us. A host extrondire. Please allow me to serve the dessert. Just set back down and how would you like your dessert?"

"I want my ice cream around the edge of the pie."

"And Sterling?"

"Mine the same way except put your finger in the ice cream, make it a little sweeter."

Ann staring at Sterling, "You always trying to stay in trouble."

Sterling looking at Milt. "Want to go fishing with me and Burt tomorrow morning."

"Don't think so, Sterling, I'm going home with my sweetie pie and spend the day with her."

"Aw Milt just in the morning, She'll still be asleep when we get back."

"Still ain't going, I'm sleeping in too."

Ann setting down in her spot staring at Sterling. Taking a bite of pie grinning. "It don't matter if he goes or not you had better not spray him again. You are responsible."

Milt said, "But I'm not going out there. I'm getting more rest, and be sure I get back to work."

Ann looking at Charlene, "before Milt and I leave I'm going to help with the cleanup."

Ann and Milt leaves after the cleanup, leaving out the door. Milt gives Charlene a hug, "thank you and Sterling for your hospitilaty. And I really enjoyed the dinner."

Charlene said, as she shut the door locking it. Walking to the gun cabinet getting her Springfield .45 auto out making sure it is loaded, along with her Smith and Wesson revolver in .357 Remington magnum. Laying them on the end table of her recliner, she bends down to Sterling, "honey I'm going to bed now, headache trying to take over. ya'll just set up and watch some television. And if ya decide to go fishing please be as quiet as possible, leaving. I sure do love you my man."

"Are you all right?"

"Well yes and no. Just don't know what is going to happen. Baby I am scared, but any thing happens tonight it won't be to you and Burt. I promise ya that. Sterling these people are more serious than you can imagine."

"Well I'm gonna get my shotgun loaded up with those buckshot, just incase they do bust in here. If I have too I'll be shooting into their faces. Hey I love you to pretty lady. Good night. Should you need anything just let me know."

Burt looking around wondering what is going on. 'Has Sterling gotten himself into something he can't get out of?'

Charlene watching Burt, "Burt don't be worried and scared. There is something going on that does not involve you nor Sterling. I can't tell you right now. But you are not in any immediate danger. Okay. And ya'll go on fishing and have a good time. Good night Burt, and I love you too."

"Good night Charlie, I love you."

Charlene waltzs on to the bedroom and lays down.

Burt and Sterling watching the base ball game, "Um Sterling, what might be going to happen?"

"I hate to tell ya, just leave it alone for now. You don't want to be drawn into this. The less ya know the better off ya, are." They finish watching the game then the news and weather. "Sterling said, standing up stretching and yawning, "Burt we better be getting some sleep, four o'clock comes early. Good night."

"Yep it sure does, I'm turning in too."

Buzzzzzzz-----buzzzzzzz---buzzzzzz, Sterling wakes up and turns the alarm off quickly. Lays back putting his hand over his forehead. 'man, that was some dream I was in. If I could just remember what it was.' Buzzzzzzz-buzzzzzz, he reaches for it one more time while setting on the edge of the bed. Le---me get up and go to the bathroom. Then wanders into the kitchen slidding his hand through the tangled hair. *Boomaloom, bom---bo-----boom, then sizz--sizzz, crack pow, the lightning lighting up the kitchen.* 'Wow! man a storm is passing through.'

Burt wanders into the kitchen, "Sterling what was that?"

"Burt a summer thunderstorm is just passing through. Hey lets get dressed and get on out to the creek. I've wanted to test the theory that lightning makes bass strike more often than the lightning itself."

"Yea Sterling, you can go out there and test any theory that strikes you. I'm going back to bed. Got to go to the bathroom right now. Flipping the bathroom light switch, lighting the room up. 'ah we still have power. That lightning strike didn't knock the power out. Hope it don't.' *Boooooma loom, boooooooma--maloom, rolling off into the North East, crack pow then the flash of lightning flickers into the window.*

Charlene wakes up, and saunters into the kitchen wrapped in her robe. "What are you two doing up at this hour? Baby I know you are not going to take him out in this weather. I woke up when you were talking about testing some theory. Then wanders into the bathroom. Coming out she turns the light off, "Sterling Baby come on back to bed and lets sunggle up close to each other. The air conditioner has gotten it rather cool in the bedroom. Be good to sleep in at least one day."

"Burt replies, "yep, ya'll keep it pretty cool in the whole house, well right now just about cold. I'm gonna get a blanket to get under. Sure wish Janie and I was at home."

Sterling turns the kitchen light off and lays down listening to the constant pattering of rain hitting the metal roof and the sizzling sound it makes through the trees. Charlene rolls over putting her hand and head on his chest. "baby I sure do love you. I really don't know what is going to happen but something is. She looks up at Sterling as he reaches down pressing his lips onto hers as she rises up futher on him.

Eight o'clock Sterling wakes up wrapped around Charlene. He lays still for a minute listening, to the light rain hitting the roof and ground. Then he gets up and returns to the bathroom. Wandering into the kitchen with his pajama bottom on and robe wrapped around himself. he puts a pot of coffee on, and sets down at the table while it brews. Then rises up and walks to the brewer and pours himself a cup and quietly saunters back to the table. He opens his Bible up and begins his study and devotion. Charlene enters into the kitchen and pours a cup and sets down. Good morning baby."

"Good morning baby. He reaches his hand out onto the top of her head and shakes it. Laughing, "ain't you a sight. Yep a very pretty sight baby."

She grabs his hand pulling it off smiling, "you are a sight to look at too. Coffee sure is good. Hey how about pancakes, scrambled eggs and bacon for breakfast."

"yes, that sounds great."

"Burt still sleeping?"

Burt walks into the kitchen, "not any more, coffe sure smells good."

Charlene said, "set down Burt I'll get you a cup. I'm going to start cooking breakfast. Here ya go," setting the steaming cup on the table. What ya'll got planned now that the weather has turned rainy?"

Sterling answers, "well not much. Wasn't thinking about rain."

Burt said, "no mention of rain in the weather forcast last night either. I'm really surprised at this."

Ring ring, ringaling, Sterling answers the phone. "Hello, oh yes Jan, he is right here. Getting ready for breakfast. Here he is." handing Burt the phone.

"Hello."

"Good morning Burt, know who this is?"

"Why I sure do, I love you so much Janie. I'm ready for you to come on back home, sugar pie, honey bunch sweet bread."

"Burt honey we are on the plane high in the sky flying straight to Jackson. It'll be later this afternoon."

"Janie, sweet bread, let me know about an hour or so before your plane lands. I'll get in my pickup and ride up to Jackson and meet you. Well have dinner at the Golden Corral or Out back. Hey maybe the Lonestar."

"All right honey I'll call you back and have your mind made up about dinner. I'll be ready to go out with you. I've got to go now. Call later. I love you."

"I love you too, Honey bunch, goodbye."

Charlene said, "Aint you such a romantic Burt? Come on to the table. I have breakfast ready."

Burt sets down at the table with a wide grin and red faced. "Why, Charlene you and Sterling say stuff like that to each other all the time." Pouring syrup over his stack of pancakes. "Man this looks good."

Charlene said, "hold on Burt, the man of the house has to give thanks for the food we are about to eat."

After the a-men, Burt cuts into his stack of three pancakes and takes a bite. "Wow! Charlie, you are a great cook."

"Thank you Burt, Just eat all you can, I have plenty."

Booooooooommmmmmaaaaaalooooooooom, bo0-b00-ma-ma-am-maloooom. Sterling said, as the lights flickered. "Looks like another storm is coming. Booooom maloooom, the red flicker of lightning lights up the windows as Burt glances out.

Burt said, "Well looks like a day to stay inside. I hope these storms clears out before Jan's flight arrives."

Sterling said, "aw Burt I would'nt worry about that too much. Those jets can fly through anything. But anyway I'm sure by the time it arrives most of this bad weather will be gone. How about another cup of coffee. I'm going to see what is on television, and maybe nap some. Charlene thank you for cooking this morning. I'll clean the dishes later. Won't be long."

"Sterling I' will get the dishes okay. You two just go into the living room and watch television or nap. I'm feeliing good right now. Maybe we can go out later today."

"Sure we will. catch a dinner and movie?"

Burt said, while rising from the table, "When Janie calls me again, I'm heading on to Jackson to greet her when she gets off the plane with Beth and June. Sure do miss those three."

Charlene responds. "Yea I know you do Burt. But they'll be home soon and things will be back to normal. Just don't listen to Sterling on some things."

"ha, ha, ha" Sterling laughing, "hey Burt it's quit raining wanna lets go out to the creek?"

Burt casts a glance at Sterling, "Sterling if you want to go fishing that bad, just do it. I'm staying put right here until I get that phone call. Oh and if ya'll leave before I do then I'll lock the door when I leave. Yep, me and Jan, Beth and June are going home."

One forty five, riing, ringaaaaling, ringling, Sterling said, "answer the phne Burt it's probably for you."

Burt just gets to the phone answering, "hello."

The sweet happy high pitched voice on the other end said, "Are you my handsome nearly bald husband? Do you have a couple of children you'd like to see?"

"Oh, hi Janie, you betch ya, I'm looking forward to seeing ya'll once again."

"Well Burt, we will be landing in just a little over an hour. Are you still coming to meet us at the airport?"

"I sure am, I'll be on my way in a few minutes. I'm going to spruce up a little and get to smelling really good."

Sterling in the back ground said. "Oh yea, I have just the right stuff for ya."

Janie exclaimed, "Do'nt let him spray you with anything Burt! I don't care if it is his personal favorite colonge."

Burt said while lookng at Sterling. "Janie sweet bread, I'm not going to let that happen. I have my own personal favorite, and you like it too. My British Sterling."

"oh yes Burt, honey I've always like that scent on you. As long as it isn't Sterling Silver."

"Nooooo, nooooooo, I won't even consider that, honey bunch."

All right we are excited about being back with you honey. Just stay fresh and clean. And be safe driving to the airport. Hey Burt I love you.

"I love you too sugar pie. Good bye."

Sterling looking at Burt, "you're fixing to head out huh."

"Yep in a few minutes, I'll shave and get the British Sterling on and head on up there."

Afterwards as he is about to walk out to his pickup, "well Sterling, Charlie, I do appreciate your hospitality. I'm going on up there. Don't want to get in a rush because of the rain."

Charlene said in a chuckling voice and smiling. "Burt you are most welcome, so be careful driving." Shutting the door she looks at Sterling, "Well honey the rain seems to be getting harder again. How about lets getting a barbeque plate and staying in this afternoon. Got to get up a little early for church tomorrow morning anyway. Go down to the church and pray before ayone arrives and practice on the choir special."

"That'll be good with me baby."

"I'll call it in, what would you want?"

"I'll have the rib plate with baked beans and potato salad. I'll go and get them."

CHAPTER 12

DEMORALIZING DEMONS

Sterling returns with the two dinners. Exiting his pickup quickly making a dash for the porch trying to keep from getting too wet. Shaking water off as he enters the door, "I'm back, as Charlene paces quickly in a fright to the front door. "Oh Sterling you scared me. Wasn't expecting you back so soon."

"Oh I didn't mean to scare you baby. They had our dinners ready when I got there. Didn't have to wait like I usually do."

"Thats okay honey, I'm just a little jumpy because of the news I've received. I am really concerned and worried for you baby. And tonight would be the kind of night they would strike." She walks to the door opens it and looks around the area and then shuts and locks it.

By the time the ten o'clock news and weather goes off the rain has subsided. Sterling said. "Well I hope this rain is gone for a while. The yard is really soaked now, and the grass is really going to grow."

"I know that Sterling you'll just have to get out there and ride that mower. Hey it is bed time. Set the clock for six. I'll get up and get breakfast cooked and then go down to the church."

Okay baby, I'm right behind you. Got to get my teeth brushed first. That was a good plate of ribs tonight. Never know when they will be tough or tender."

"Yes, its why I got the chicken plate. it is always good." She grabs her Springfield 1911 .45 and carries it to the bed room. And Sterling stands his Remington 1187 auto shotgun loaded with the buckshot loads in the corner by the bed. Then walks into the bathroom and brushes his teeth and returns to the bed. Laying down Charlene looks at him and smiles. Thinking *'as much as I love this man, he doesn't know. He thinks he'll have time to get that long barreled gun into play. Well he may not know it but he won't. Anyway he is my hero. I believe he would give his life for me.'* "Sterling, my man, my hero, I so much love you baby good night."

"Good night, my pretty lady. I love you too."

"Sterling how about turning over on your other side."

"okay," She puts her arm around him as best she can and pulls him in close. Smiles and shuts her eyes.

Sunday night after the worship services, they walk together into their home. She spins around, "Oh Sterling the worship services were really great weren't they. The choir did so well. Even Mister, Brown finally gave a plesant comment as to how much they have improved in these past couple of years I've been here. I just love it when people like him offer comments of encouragement. You know, I just praise the Lord."

Charlene baby, you are a professional. And the choir did sound great today. Hey they always do, they don't want to let you down."

"And Mrs. Rose accepted the solo part in a song with the choir. I'll be working on it with her most of this week. We'll do it next Sunday. So please Sterling in your devotionals pray for us, epecially Rose."

"Why you, know I will. It is going to be great."

"Hey baby, how about a slice of pie before turning in for the night. Sure would be good. Just set down and I'll bring it to you." She returns with a couple of sausers with apple pie and sets down next to Sterling handing him the small plate.

"Honey this is good. Well might as well set up and watch the news and weather ain't but another forty minutes. Then go to bed."

Taking his plate, "would you like another slice?"

"If you'll slice it small." She brings him another slice, and sets down beside him, putting her hand on his thigh.

"Baby things are really quite. I wonder if those people have forgotten about me or can't find me. I just hope they have forgotten me, or thinks I died in that shoot out. It would be good if I never hear from them. But if I ever knew those couple of men I was wheeling and dealing with, they should be out there somewhere. Waiting for the right moment. They are bloodhounds on a trail."

Swallowing down a bite of the pie. "Maybe we won't have to deal with them. You know it has been over twenty five years ago. But in case they are tracking you down, I'll try to be more alert of my surroundings. Because that means they are after me too."

"Baby just be careful. Please let me know if you see or hear anything suspicous. I won't really like you leaving alone for work tomorrow morning."

"I'll be alright. Got to go any way."

"I know baby, But right now I'm heading to the bed. Need to be at the office by eight o'clock.

"I'm coming on to bed too. Got to get up early." Laying down, Sterling turns over kissing her good night, then places his arm around and pulling her in close to him. She sighs in comfort, closing her eyes. "I love you too pretty lady."

Softly she whispers, "I love you my man."

Sitting at a table in the break room eating his tuna fish salad sandwich, waiting for a chance to get the break room phone. *I hope he will get off the phone before break is over, I would call Charlene and speak with her a minute.*'

Shortly he hangs the phone up and Sterling gets to it and calls the church Office. The voice comes on and a big smile comes over his face. "Hopewell Baptist church. Enter to worship, depart to serve. This is Charlene may I be of assistance to you?"

"Hey baby, Its me just calling to check on on you."

"Oh hi Sterling my man how is working going today?"

"Oh its here, nothing exciting to look forward to but more work."

"Honey are you okay? Sounds like something is wrong."

"Oh I'm I'm alright, just thinking about you."

"I'm leaving the office around two today. It has been a really busy morning. Been counseling a number of people from depression to those who are trying to decide if they want to start coming here. And sickness. You know honey I just wish I could reach out and touch those people and say in the name of Jesus Christ you are healed. I just can't really get a grasp as to why it won't happen. I have the faith and compassion for it."

"Oh I know it, and I'm going to show you something in the Gospels that likely tells us the why."

"I sure would like to see it. Hey when I get off I'll meet you at the plant and we'll have an early dinner somewhere."

"I'm all for that baby. Well the bell is about to ring for us to return to work. See you here later. I love you pretty lady."

"I love you my man, be there later."

As she leaves the church office, swinging by Reverend Stockon's office, knocking and peeping in. Reverend stockon said. "You gone Sister?"

"yes, I'm through for the day. Going to get Sterling when he gets off and go for a early dinner. See you Wednesday evening. Oh and please help me pray for those people I've encountered and visited with today." Then noticing a large yellow envelope on his desk.

"Sure will sister Silver. See you Wednesday."

Monday morning Sterling checks on Charlene before leaving for the day's work. All is all right he slips out the door, and drives up the highway to the plant. Arriving home in the afternoon, he enterns the house, I'm hooooooo-me pretty lady." She rushes to the living room meeting him with a hug and kiss. "have a good day at work today?"

"Yes it was a good day. "In a few minutes I'm heading out to let the lawn mower drag me around the yard for a while."

"Honey have you heard anything from our campers lately?"

"Naw, haven't, I guess they are still catching up with each other."

"Well I'll call Ann and Janie tomorrow, Better-n-that I'll go a visit with them. Hey don't be out there too long you know how hot it is. I'm going to fry chicken livers and make gravy for rice."

"Sounds good for me baby. I'm headed to the lawn mower, I can just feel it shaking from the fear of working for me."

"Yea, right Sterling. Be careful my man, I'm gone to cook."

Getting out of the shower, he walks in to the kitchen. "You ready to eat honey?"

"Ah yes, it certainly smells good as he makes his plate and sits down. Charlene brings him a glass of sweet tea and places it down beide the plate, staring at him with a playful grin. "it has ten ice cubes in it too. So I won't have to skin you baby."

When she arrives back at the table with her plate and tea, Sterling rises up and pulls her chair out. "Thank you baby, lets have the blessing, I'll pray this time." Looking up from the prayer as she cuts into a liver with the fork. "Sterling I have a meeting at the church tomorrow morning. Set the clock for me too will ya?"

"Sure will baby. Charlene I'll do the dishes for you."

"Honey you can help if you want. Hey then lets get in the bed and watch television."

Tuesday morning arriving at the church's office, entering she feels as if on a judgment seat with the church council staring at her, while the chairman opens the large yellow envelope.

"Charlene, can you explain these pictures of you, in a night club on a dance stage stripping?"

As the shock and embarrassment floods over, taking her back in time. "Um no I can't and I won't that was a long time ago. Why"

"Well we knew you were a drug enforcement agent during those times but had no idea of this."

Beginning to shake as tears wells up in her eyes thinking about Sterling and her love for him. "Well I'm going to say it one more time this was in another time. That is dead and gone. Look, I love my Lord and Savior Jesus Christ who saved me from that, and now I'm all fof a sudden back in judgment. Just where did you get those pictures?"

"A man by the name of Poco Loco dropped them off."

Staring at the pictures, 'so ole Poco loco. yep it is him. I'm fixing to have togo back there and finsh what I left years ago. Lord please help me.'

"Well Charlene we as the church council has to ask for your resignation."

Putting her face in hands she begins weeping.

To be continued

Printed in the United States
By Bookmasters